D0825678

NATIVE AMERICAN
ANIMAL STORIES

Borg

Seeing the Animals

Their eyes are
not our eyes
yet we can see
ourselves in them.

We do not walk
the ways they walk,
yet we follow
their footprints in sand.

Sometimes they come
to us, when we
hold their silence
they understand.

When they live with us
we must give them respect,
though most stay apart
like the bird which is hidden
yet touches us with its song.

Sometimes we think
that we humans can live
without them,
but we are wrong.

—Joseph Bruchac

NATIVE AMERICAN
ANIMAL STORIES

Told by *Joseph Bruchac*

from *Keepers of the Animals*
Michael J. Caduto and Joseph Bruchac

Foreword by Vine Deloria, Jr.
Illustrations by John Kahionhes Fadden
and David Kanietakeron Fadden

Fulcrum Publishing
Golden, Colorado

Copyright © 1992 Joseph Bruchac

Cover Illustration by John Kahionhes Fadden
Illustrations Copyright © 1992 John Kahionhes Fadden and
David Kanietakeron Fadden

Book design and cover colorization by Karen Groves

The map on pages xviii–xix, showing the culture regions of the Native North
American groups discussed in this book, is printed with permission of Michael J.
Caduto (© 1991). Cartography by Stacy Miller, Upper Marlboro, Maryland.

All Rights Reserved

No part of this publication may be reproduced, stored in a retrieval system or
transmitted in any form or by any means, electronic, mechanical, photocopying,
recording or otherwise without the prior written permission of the publisher.

Library of Congress Cataloging-in-Publication Data

Bruchac, Joseph
    Native American animal stories / told by Joseph Bruchac.
        p.   cm.
    "From Keepers of the animals / Michael J. Caduto and Joseph Bruchac."
    Includes bibliographical references.
    ISBN 978-1-55591-127-0
    1. Indians of North America—Legends. 2. Animals—Folklore. I. Caduto,
Michael J. Keepers of the animals. II. Title.
E98.F6B895 1992
398.2'08997—dc20   92-53040
                                                                        CIP
Printed in the United States of America
20   19   18   17   16   15   14

Fulcrum Publishing
4690 Table Mountain Drive, Suite 100
Golden, Colorado 80403
(800) 992-2908 • (303) 277-1623
www.fulcrumbooks.com

This book is dedicated to the memory of

> Louis Littlecoon Oliver, Creek poet and storyteller

> Maurice Dennis/Little Loon, Abenaki storyteller and artist

> Swift Eagle, Apache and Santo Domingo Pueblo singer, dancer and storyteller

Friends and teachers, whose voices and stories will always live in my heart.

Contents

Foreword

It is often said that we take our cues about what constitutes proper behavior from the people around us. Most probably we get most of our knowledge about the world we live in from our surroundings, although we like to pretend that, with our great colleges and universities, our massive libraries and complex computer retrieval systems, we have more access to information than did people in earlier times. The immensity of the data available to us poses a problem. How do we make this information our own in the sense of using it in a practical manner? Here we lag far behind all previous societies and may indeed be abstracting ourselves from the natural world to an alarming and self-threatening degree. With some rare exceptions, would or could any of us survive in a wholly natural setting? Or are we condemned to remain restricted within the artificial institutional universe that we have constructed?

Our knowledge of birds, animals and the natural world, when we have any ideas about them at all, is derived primarily from television, textbooks and unfortunately, from cartoons that feature cuddly and all-too-human bears, energetic roadrunners and inept coyotes. Other than in petting zoos at supermarkets and roadside cages, few of our children ever see animals, and they never see them in their natural habitats. Animal stories, therefore, are fraught with the possibility of misunderstanding unless some effort is made to provide a context in which the stories take place that is true to the natural setting and behavior of the animals.

Native North Americans saw themselves as participants in a great natural order of life, related in some fundamental manner to every other living species. It was said that each species had a particular knowledge of the universe and specific skills for living in it. Human beings had a little bit of knowledge and some basic skills, but we could not compare with any other animals as far as speed, strength, cunning and intelligence. Therefore it was incumbent on us to respect every other form of life, to learn from them as best we could the proper behavior in this world and the specific technical skills necessary to survive and prosper. Man was the youngest member of the web of life and, therefore, had to have some humility in the face of the talents and experience of other species.

Native North Americans made a point of observing the other creatures and in modeling their own behavior after them. Many of the social systems of the tribes were patterned after their observations of the birds and animals, and in those tribes that organized themselves in clans, every effort was made to follow the behavior of the clan totem animal or birds. Teaching stories for children emphasized the virtues of the animals, and children were admonished to be wise, gentle, brave, or cheerful in the same manner as certain birds and animals. Some of the tribes even developed a psychology of birds and animals, describing human personality traits as being similar to those of coyotes, beavers, elk, bears and so forth. These psychological descriptions are amazingly accurate in terms of predicting individual behavior and frequently surprise casual observers.

The technical skills of birds, animals and reptiles were such that Native North Americans could take cues from them for their own welfare. If birds consistently built nests out of certain materials, it meant that they recognized and adjusted to the fact of harsh or mild weather in a certain location. The building of beaver dams in certain parts of rivers gave information on the depth of water, its purity, the kinds of fish and other water creatures in the locale and the kinds of roots, berries and medicine roots that would be available at that place. Animal trails were carefully observed by the people because inevitably the game animals would take the shortest and easiest path through mountains, prairies and desert and would not be far from water and edible plants.

Hunting and gathering techniques also varied according to the information received from observing animals. A surplus of some small animals would indicate the sparsity of population of their natural enemies and a paucity would indicate that these predators were in abundance in the area. A determination of the edibility of plants was obtained from watching animals; the presence of medicine roots was often indicated by the presence of the animals who primarily used these roots and had passed their knowledge on to humans. Gradually, as the people improved their knowledge of the relationships between the various life forms that inhabited the lands they developed, a species-specific pharmacology evolved, so that they could treat birds and animals for diseases specific to them. Thus a medicine man or woman was credited with having "elk," "deer," "horse" or other kinds of medicine and could cure these animals.

Much of the religious ceremony and ritual of the tribes was derived from information provided to them by birds, animals and reptiles. The famous Hopi "Snake Dance" enabled the people to live in an arid high plateau desert because the snakes could bring water to assist the Hopi in growing corn. In almost every ritual of the tribes, other species participated as full partners. Some of these ceremonies involved the bird or animal in sacrificing its life in order to ensure that the ceremony was properly done. Modern people have a difficult time understanding the nature of these ceremonies or how, after an eagle has been killed in a ceremony, one can look skyward and see eagles circling the site as if they were giving their approval of what had taken place.

The relationship was so close between humans and other forms of life that it was believed that humans could take the shape of the birds and animals for some time after their deaths. Thus it was not uncommon, following the death of an old person, to see a hawk or woodpecker circling the camp or village. Owls sometimes gathered in large numbers on the approaching death of a medicine man. I have personally seen a gathering of nearly three hundred owls on the prairie where there is hardly a blade of grass to sustain life, so I know that many of these stories are to be taken literally and do not merely illustrate a teaching lesson.

Interestingly, many tribes had classifications among the birds and animals that enabled them to explain complicated relationships and provided them with additional knowledge not obtainable from any one species. Thus the Plains Indians saw a grand distinction between two-legged and four-legged creatures. Among the two-leggeds were humans, birds and bears. Bears were included because when feeding, they often stand on two legs. Since the two-leggeds are responsible for helping to put the natural world back into balance when it becomes disordered, birds, bears and humans share a responsibility to participate in healing ceremonies and indeed the cumulative knowledge of these three groups is primarily one of healing.

Over the centuries, certain birds, animals and reptiles and particular human families became very closely associated. They were, in most respects, one intimate family and consequently these families depended upon their animal relatives to warn them of impending dangers or crises of a transitional nature. It is not uncommon to see a family animal in the vicinity of a Native North American home or to find unusual bird and animal appearances happening among some native families. Only the most knowledgeable medicine men or women know the depth of these relationships, but they are very sophisticated, and many people make decisions based on the appearance of the animal people who signal whether a proposed course of action is proper or not.

The stories in this book present some of the basic perspectives that Native North American parents, aunts and uncles use to teach the young. They are phrased in terms that modern youngsters can understand and appreciate. Much of the information about the weather, the particularities of the land and the continuing relationships with birds and animals is not included because we no longer live in a natural setting. Nevertheless, at the most basic level of gathering information, these tales have much to tell us. They enable us to understand that while birds and animals appear to be similar in thought processes to humans, that is simply the way we represent them in our stories. But other creatures do have thought processes, emotions, personal relationships and many of the experiences that we have in our lives. We must carefully accord these other creatures the respect that they deserve and the right to live without unnecessary harm. Wanton killings of different animals by some hunters and sportsmen are completely outside the traditional way that native people have treated other species, and if these stories can help develop in young people a strong sense of the wonder of other forms of life, this sharing of Native North American knowledge will certainly have been worth the effort.

—Vine Deloria, Jr.

All Are My Relations:
Native People and Animals

As you read these stories of humans and animals, it would be good to bear in mind from the very start that there is a difference between the way the Native peoples of this continent see animals and the way animals are viewed by most of the western world. The western world sees animals as beasts—beasts of burden, beasts to be hunted, beasts to be feared. Animals, in general, are to be owned, used or hunted. If they are not useful to human beings in some way, they are to be eliminated. Seldom, apart from a few nature mystics such as St. Francis of Assisi, do we hear the animals referred to as our relatives.

Yet to the Native people of North America, the birds and fish, the snakes and animals, all those crawling, swimming, flying, two-legged and four-legged beings were regarded as relations. Perhaps the most dramatic example of that difference between the European and the North American Native points of view about animals can be seen in the Miwok story of creation which begins this book. Instead of the earth being created by a deity whose shape is the same as that of human beings, Earth comes into being through the thoughts and wishes of two animals—Silver Fox and Coyote. Such an earth, therefore, is a very different place from a planet that is dominated by the thoughts and wishes of human beings alone.

Like traditional peoples in many other parts of the world, the Native people of North America do not make a separation between the world of the sacred and the world we call "everyday." There is, as with Christianity, Judaism or Islam, a general belief in the existence of a God who is the ultimate Creator. This God, however, is not seen primarily (if at all) in human form. Most often God is referred to as a Great Mystery or a Great Spirit, one whose essence is not exclusively male or female, human or animal, but in and of all things. The word for this Great Spirit in Lakota is Wakan Tanka; in Abenaki it is Ktsi Nwaskw, in Ojibway it is Gitchee Manitou. The presence of the Great Mystery is everywhere. Everything around us is alive and contains a part of that spiritual presence of the Creator. And this Great Spirit cares equally for all parts of Creation—humans, animals, plants and stones.

Most Native people of North America perceive the natural state of the world as a state of balance. We are part of a great circle and we are not more important than the plants or the animals or the rocks. Animals and plants are beings equal to humans. In some cases, they are described as ancestors, and stories of animals becoming people and people becoming animals are common. Animals, whether they are connected to people or not, have their own families and traditions. And, along with human beings, they are part of a world that is meant to be in balance.

When we humans become sick, Native people perceive that it is because we have lost the balance, and we must restore that balance to regain our health in a world in which everything is alive, in which the presence of the Creator is everywhere. Prayer and ceremonies that involve the patient's entire community (a community that goes beyond the human family) became important elements in restoring that balance. Living in a way that shows respect to all of creation is vitally important. (This concept is familiar to contemporary ecologists who state—from a scientific point of view—that the future health of our planet and ourselves may be measured by how well our animal brothers and sisters are doing.)

The Iroquois, for example, traditionally diagnosed different kinds of illness, including sickness that comes because a hunter has not shown respect for the animals he has killed. In several of the stories in this book from different parts of North America, we see the disastrous results of a lack of respect. In the Tlingit tale of "The Salmon Boy," for example, the central character can only learn and restore balance by dying and having his soul reborn as a salmon. When respect is shown, however, as in the Cree story of "How the People Hunted the Moose," the animals will even go so far as to sacrifice their bodies to help human beings live. Both of these tales also point out an important principle in Native religious beliefs—that humans and animals have souls and that those souls survive the death of the body.

The treatment for illness among Native people of North America is, of course, not limited only to prayer. It can include sweat baths, massage, exercise and manipulation of the joints, and the careful use of prepared medicines. These medicines may come from either animals or plants. One Seneca story tells of a good hunter whose name was Red Hand. Red Hand always showed respect for animals. When he was killed in battle and left lying in the forest, the animals found his body. While the bear embraced him to keep him warm, each of the other animals contributed a small part of themselves to make a special medicine that brought Red Hand back to life. That medicine was still in use among the Iroquois people in the 1800s and, according to the writings of Iroquois ethnologist Arthur Parker, is called the "Little Water Medicine."

The lives of the people depended upon the animals who have provided, as the stories eloquently document, human beings not only with food and clothing, but also with social structures, dances and songs and ethical principles. Thus, the lives of the "animal people" (as the Native people of North America so often express it) and the human people are as connected and inseparable from each other in tradition as is the air around us, the breath of life which is shared by humans and animals alike. And we are always learning from the animals. They help us in so many ways.

Perhaps I can explain it, in part, by telling a story of my own about the animals.

It was an October day. The long slanting sunlight of autumn was bright on the maple leaves, but my heart felt dull and heavy. It had been a difficult day. I was working that year as a teacher in a college program inside a prison and it seemed as if the iron and stone of the prison had come home with me. Even though that October day was my birthday, I was in no mood for celebration.

"I'm going for a walk up into the Woods," I said to my wife, Carol.

The Woods have been in our family for six generations now, as far as those records on paper kept in the town courthouse go. But the woods have been in my family's blood, on the Indian side, for much longer than that. They've been part of our dreaming for as far back as memory can reach—and we remember back a long, long way. (And because we dream of the future, too, the Woods are now protected—thanks to my mother—in perpetuity. In 1991 she signed over all development rights to the Saratoga Land Conservancy in a conservation easement.)

The Woods are just across the road from our house. It is an area of forest and old fields that was larger in the past—before housing developments and the building of new roads—but it still contains almost ninety acres. There are century-old stands of pine and hemlock and mixed hardwoods. There are two swamps and two brooks that flow through, feeding into the Kayaderosseras Creek, which is itself a tributary of the great Hudson River. There are three old hayfields that we do not harvest but cut once each fall so that there will be places for the wild flowers and the animals and birds that thrive on the edges between meadow and forest. If they were not cut each year, those fields soon would be filled up by the honey locusts and sumacs and fire cherry that reclaimed the now-wooded parts of the property where my great-grandfather pastured his cows. Only half-buried stone walls mark the boundaries of those long-gone grazing lands, deep under the canopy of hundred-year-old hemlocks and wide-branched pines.

I took a deep breath as I crossed Middle Grove Road into the woods, and my feet felt the give of sod underfoot after the hardness of asphalt. I followed the trail that parallels Bell Brook at the field's edge. A hundred yards further I turned left, passing under old dead elms. The long shoots of blackberry bushes tugged at my sleeves, and beechnuts and acorns cracked underfoot. It had been a good year for mast, and the places where squirrels and chipmunks had been digging could be seen in the dirt and leaves. Bell Brook was flowing deep from the autumn rains and as I crossed it, coming to the little clearing where the sweat lodge stood stripped of its blankets, I felt a little more of the weight of the world fall away from me. I spoke some of the old words for thanks by the cold fire pit and walked on up the hill toward the Middle Field.

I entered the Middle Field through the almost invisible break in the honey-suckle bushes and multifloral roses bordering most of the eastern and southern edges of the field. The colors of fall-browned grass and painted leaves washed away the sad sameness of prison grays that had been filling my eyes. I came into the field and continued along its eastern edge.

Always walk the edge of a field, my grandfather said. *Keep your feet quiet, your mind still and your eyes open.*

Suddenly, just as I reached the corner of the field where a small hickory hung one bough low over the path and the ranks of sumacs from the unmowed northern edge of the field were thickest, a bird burst up and out of the little trees. It came straight at me, its wings almost brushing my hair. It passed so close that I heard the whit-whit-shu-it of its wings through the air, felt the wind of its passing on my face. It was a wood thrush. Its spotted chest filled my sight for that one second and hung like a ghost image before my eyes after it was past. My heart beat quicker. I felt I had been given a blessing. But there was more.

Something wove its way toward me through the small sumacs—a small yellow dog. As it took two more steps and came out of the trees into the matted grass, I knew it belonged to no one but itself. One paw raised, its head lifted, it looked straight into my eyes without fear. A red fox.

I looked back at it, only ten yards away. *It's going to turn and run.* But it didn't. It stood still, eyes on mine. As it stood there, an old song came to me. It came not just into my mind, but into my throat and lungs and heart. It was a song I'd learned from an Apache elder named Swift Eagle. Swifty was one of my best teachers, not in a school, but during those times when we sat or walked together and I listened to his stories. His song was in me and around me and I could hear it. The fox pricked up its ears toward me, and I knew that it heard the song, too. That was when I realized that I was singing that song. I sang and the fox began to walk. It walked toward me, and there was a look on its face that I understood. Six feet away from me, it sat down on its haunches and yawned. The sun was bright and its coat looked orange now, as orange as the sumac leaves. I stopped singing and the fox cocked its head up at me as if to ask, *Well, isn't there another verse to that song?* So I sang again. I sang and the fox listened and the sun shone on both of us and the sunshine was in my heart.

To this day, I have only to think of that moment to realize how great the gift was that fox gave to me—a gift of sudden awareness that made me stop to appreciate the beauty of this earth and to be thankful for this great gift of life we share. Our Creator made it to be this way. So it is said in the Iroquois Thanksgiving Prayer, a prayer to be spoken at the start of any gathering. Part of that prayer, which gives thanks for all things, reminds us that our Creator made it so that there should be animals of many kinds. Some of these animals would be companions to the people. Some would help us by allowing us to use their bodies to provide food and clothing for the people, but only as long as we respect them and give them thanks and take only what is needed for the people to survive. Never more and never with cruelty. The animals have their own families and nations, and we must recognize them. We must respect them as brothers and sisters. Without the animals, our human lives would indeed be hard and lonely on this earth. So, in that prayer, we greet and thank the animals.

This is what I want us to remember—to respect the animals, to greet and thank them and to keep them in our minds and hearts. So I tell the story of my walk that day. So I tell these stories of animals from many different Native nations, to respect the animals, for all are my relations. Let us give them greetings and thanks.

—Joseph Bruchac

BERING
SEA

ARCTIC
OCEAN

WESTERN ALEUT

EASTERN ALEUT

NORTH
ALASKAN
INUIT-INUPIAQ (ESKIMO)

BERING
STRAIT
INUIT-INUPIAQ
(ESKIMO)

KOTZEBUE
INUIT-INUPIAQ
(ESKIMO)

NORTHERN
INTERIOR
INUIT-INUPIAQ (ESKIMO)

GENERAL CENTRAL YUPIK (ESKIMO)

CENTRAL ALASKAN YUPIK (ESKIMO)

Koyukon

MACKENZIE (ESKIMO) INUIT

Tanaina

Tanana

Kutchin

Han

Chugach

Ahtna

COPPER
INUIT
(ESKIMO)

Hare

Yellowknife

CEN

Tutchone

S U B A

INLAND
TLINGIT

Kaska

Slavey

Dogrib

Chipewyan

TLINGIT

Tahltan

Sekani

Beaver

HAIDA

TSIMSHIAN

WESTERN WOODS CREE

Carrier

Chilcotin

Sarcee

PACIFIC NORTHWEST

Bella
Bella
Bella
Coola

KWAKIUTL

PLAINS CREE

NOOTKA

SQUAMISH

PLAIN
ANISHIN

Lummi

QUILEUTE

Nis-
qually

PLATEAU

Colville

Siksika
(Blackfoot)

Klickitat

Kalispel

Flathead
(Salish)

Gros
Ventre
(Atsina)

Assiniboin
(Stoney)

Multnomah

NEZ
PERCE

PACIFIC
OCEAN

Klamath

Yurok

Modoc

ACHUMAWI

NORTHERN
PAIUTE
(PAVIOTSO)

SHOSHONE-
BANNOCK

ABSAROKE
(CROW)

Mandan
LAKOTA (SIOU

Pomo

Maidu

GREAT

Gosiute

WIND
RIVER
SHOSHONE

Northern
Cheyenne

TETON

DAKOT

MIWOK

WESTERN
SHOSHONE

BASIN

UTES

Northern
Paiute
(Paviotso)

PONC

PAWN

Yokuts

Chu-
mash

PAIUTE

Arapaho

Southern Paiute

WEST COAST

Serrano

Canyon
de Chelly

Havasupai

HOPI

DINE
(NAVAJO)

JICARILLA
APACHE

KIOWA

KI
AP

Walapai

ZUNI

PUEBLO

Ipai

Yavapai

WESTERN
APACHE

APACHE

COMANCHE

PAPAGO

CHIRICAHUA
APACHE

MESCALERO
APACHE

Upper Pima

SOUTHWEST

Lipan

YAQUI

LEGEND

———— BOUNDARIES OF CULTURAL AREAS

CREE   NATIVE AMERICAN GROUPS DISCUSSED IN
        BOOK (CAPITAL LETTERS)

Arapaho OTHER NATIVE AMERICAN GROUPS
         (INCLINED AND LOWER CASE LETTERS)

- - - - NATIONAL BOUNDARIES

········· STATE AND PROVINCIAL BOUNDARIES

CARTOGRAPHY BY STACY MILLER, UPPER MARLBORO, MD.
COPYRIGHT © 1991 MICHAEL J. CADUTO.

SCALE

0 100 200   400 STATUTE
                        MILES

BAFFIN
BAY

Iglulik

DAVIS STRAIT

BAFFINLAND
INUIT (ESKIMO)

G
I
C

(SKIMO)
Iglulingmiut

LABRADOR
SEA

(SATLIRMIUT
SOUTHAMPTON INUIT)
(ESKIMO)

LABRADOR INUIT
(ESKIMO)

HUDSON
BAY

Montagnais

Nashapi

WEST
MAIN
CREE

EAST
CREE

GULF OF
ST. LAWRENCE

I

MICMAC

ANISHINABE

WAY or CHIPPEWA)

Algonquin

Nipissing

MALISEET
PASSAMAQUODDY

WABANAKI PEOPLES

ASTERN

HAUDENOSAUNEE
(IROQUOIS)

Huron
(Wyandot)

ABENAKI
PENOBSCOT

PENNACOOK

Menominee

Potawatomi
Sauk

Neutral

Erie

Massachuset

Wampanoag

guukie

Winnebago

Fox
Kickapoo

Munsee

Narragansett
Mohegan, Pequot

WOOD-
Miami

Shawnee

Delaware (Leni
Lenape)

Illinois

Nanticoke

Powhatan

LAND

CHEROKEE

TUSCARORA

East Coast Algonquians

aw *Chickasaw*

Catawba

Muskogee (Creek)

SOUTHEAST

CHOCTAW

atchez

Seminole

F OF MEXICO

ATLANTIC

OCEAN

✦ NATIVE ✦
NORTH AMERICA

Introduction

"Let's make the world."

❖

Silver Fox and Coyote Create Earth

Back then, Silver Fox was the only one living. There was no earth, only water. Silver Fox walked along through the fog, feeling lonely. So she began to sing:

> I want to meet someone,
> I want to meet someone,
> I want to meet someone,
> I want to meet someone.

So she sang and then she met Coyote.

"I thought I was going to meet someone," Silver Fox said. "Where are you traveling?"

"Where are you traveling?" Coyote said. "Why are you traveling like this?"

"I am traveling because I am lonely," Silver Fox said.

"I am also wandering around," said Coyote.

"Then it is better for two people to travel together," Silver Fox said.

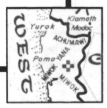

Then, as they traveled, Silver Fox spoke. "This is what I think," Silver Fox said. "Let's make the world."

"How will we do that?" Coyote said.

"We will sing the world," said Silver Fox.

So the two of them began to sing and to dance. They danced around in a circle and Silver Fox thought of a clump of sod. Let it come, Silver Fox thought, and then that clump of sod was there in Silver Fox's hands. Silver Fox threw it down into the fog and they kept on singing and dancing.

"Look down," Silver Fox said, "do you see something there below us?"

"I see something," Coyote said, "but it is very small."

"Then let us close our eyes and keep dancing and singing," said Silver Fox. And that was what they did. They danced and sang and beneath them Earth took shape.

"Look down now," Silver Fox said.

Coyote looked down. "I see it," said Coyote. "It is very big now. It is big enough."

Then the two of them jumped down onto Earth. They danced and sang and stretched it out even more. They made everything on Earth, the valleys and the mountains and the rivers and the lakes, the pines and the cedars and the birds and the animal people. That was what they did way back then.

So the two of them began to sing and to dance.

How the People Hunted the Moose

One night, a family of moose was sitting in the lodge. As they sat around the fire, a strange thing happened. A pipe came floating in through the door. Sweet-smelling smoke came from the long pipe and it circled the lodge, passing close to each of the Moose People. The old bull moose saw the pipe but said nothing, and it passed him by. The cow moose said nothing, and the pipe passed her by also. So it passed by each of the Moose People until it reached the youngest of the young bull moose near the door of the lodge.

"You have come to me," he said to the pipe. Then he reached out and took the pipe and started to smoke it.

"My son," the old moose said, "you have killed us. This is a pipe from the human beings. They are smoking this pipe now and asking for success in their hunt. Now, tomorrow, they will find us. Now, because you smoked their pipe, they will be able to get us."

"I am not afraid," said the young bull moose. "I can run faster than any of those people. They cannot catch me."

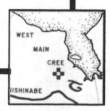

"You have
come to me,"
he said to
the pipe.

But the old bull moose said nothing more.

When the morning came, the Moose People left their lodge. They went across the land looking for food. But as soon as they reached the edge of the forest, they caught the scent of the hunters. It was the time of year when there is a thin crust on the snow and the moose found it hard to move quickly.

"These human hunters will catch us," said the old cow moose. "Their feet are feathered like those of the grouse. They can walk on top of the snow."

Then the Moose People began to run as the hunters followed them. The young bull moose who had taken the pipe ran off from the others. He was still sure he could outrun the hunters. But the hunters were on snowshoes, and the young moose's feet sank into the snow. They followed him until he tired, and then they killed him. After they had killed him, they thanked him for smoking their pipe and giving himself to them so they could survive. They treated his body with care, and they soothed his spirit.

That night, the young bull moose woke up in his lodge among his people. Next to his bed was a present given him by the human hunters. He showed it to all of the others.

"You see," he said. "It was not a bad thing for me to accept the long pipe the human people sent to us. Those hunters treated me with respect. It is right for us to allow the human beings to catch us."

And so it is to this day. Those hunters who show respect to the moose are always the ones who are successful when they hunt.

This is a pipe from the human beings.

Creation

So Grandmother Spider gathered all of the living creatures around her.

How Grandmother Spider Named the Clans

After Tawa, the Sky God, and Grandmother Spider had made Earth and all of the things upon it, Tawa went back up into the heavens. Grandmother Spider remained with the animals and all of the people there in the four great caves of the underworld. It was left to Grandmother Spider to put things on Earth into order. So Grandmother Spider gathered all of the living creatures around her. She began to separate the people into the different Indian nations, telling them how it would be from then on for them. So it was that she made the Ute and the Zuni and the Comanche and the Pueblo people and the Hopi and all of the others. She named them and from then on they knew their names. So too she gave all of the animals their names so that they also would know who they were.

Then Grandmother Spider saw that life would not be good for the many animals and people there in the darkness of the underworld. With her two grandsons, the Hero Twins, beside her, she led the animals and the people up out of the four caverns. She led them till they came to an opening into the world above. They came out there next to the Colorado River in the place where the people still go to gather salt. As

they came out, the turkey dragged his tail in the mud and his tail has been black-tipped ever since then.

Grandmother Spider sent the mourning dove ahead to find good places for the people to settle, places where there were springs and good soil for corn. Then Grandmother Spider separated the people into clans. She chose one animal to lead each of those groups of people and from then on those people carried the name of that animal. So it was that the Snake Clan and the Antelope Clan, the Mountain Lion Clan and the Deer Clan and the other clans came to be among the Hopi. The people each followed their clan animal and when they came to the place to build their homes, there they settled and there they live to this day.

Then Grandmother Spider separated the people into clans.

How the Spider Symbol Came to the People

From the earliest days when they came together on this earth, the Osage people have been divided into two groups. These groups were the Sky People and the Earth People. The nine clans of the Sky People always lived in the northern half of the village. The fifteen clans of the Earth People lived in the southern half of the village. These clans looked to the animals to be their teachers, to serve as symbols for them to live strong lives. Each clan had more than one animal as its symbol. One of these clans was called the Isolated Earth People. This is the story of how the spider became one of the symbols of that clan.

One day, the chief of the Isolated Earth People was hunting in the forest. He was not just hunting for game, he was also hunting for a symbol to give life to his people, some great and powerful animal that would show itself to him and teach him an important lesson. As he hunted, he came upon the tracks of a huge deer. The chief became very excited.

"Grandfather Deer," he said, "surely you are going to show yourself to me. You are going to teach me a lesson and become one of the symbols of my people."

Then the spider
spoke to the
man.

Then the chief began to follow the deer's tracks. His eyes were on nothing else as he followed those tracks and he went faster and faster through the forest. Suddenly, the chief ran right into a huge spider's web that had been strung between the trees across the trail. It was so large and strong that it covered his eyes and made him stumble. When he got back up to his feet, he was very angry. He struck at the spider, which was sitting at the edge of the web, but the spider dodged aside and climbed out of reach. Then the spider spoke to the man.

"Grandson," the spider said, "why do you run through the woods looking at nothing but the ground? Why do you act as if you are blind?"

The chief felt foolish, but he felt he had to answer the spider. "I was following the tracks of the great deer," the chief said. "I am seeking a symbol to give life and strength to my people."

"I can be such a symbol," said the spider.

"How could you give strength to my people?" said the chief. "You are small and weak and I didn't even see you as I followed the great deer."

"Grandson," said the spider, "look upon me. I am patient. I watch and I wait. Then all things come to me. If your people learn this, they will be strong indeed."

The chief saw that it was so. Thus the spider became one of the symbols of the Osage people.

Celebration

*Something
unusual was
happening.*

The Rabbit Dance

L ong ago, a group of hunters were out looking for game. They had seen no sign of animals, but they went slowly and carefully through the forest, knowing that at any moment they might find something. Just ahead of them was a clearing. The leader of the hunters held up his hand for the others to pause. He thought he had seen something. All of the men dropped down on their stomachs and crept up to the clearing's edge to see what they could see. What they saw amazed them. There, in the center of the clearing, was the biggest rabbit any of them had ever seen. It seemed to be as big as a small bear!

One of the hunters slowly began to raise his bow. A rabbit as large as that one would be food enough for the whole village. But the leader of the men held out his hand and made a small motion that the man with the bow understood. He lowered his weapon. Something unusual was happening. It was best to just watch and see what would happen next.

The rabbit lifted its head and looked toward the men. Even though they were well hidden on the other side of the

clearing, it seemed as if that giant rabbit could see them. But the rabbit did not take flight. Instead, it just nodded its head. Then it lifted one of its feet and thumped the ground. As soon as it did so, other rabbits began to come into the clearing. They came from all directions and, like their chief, they paid no attention to the hunters.

Now the big rabbit began to thump its foot against the ground in a different way. Ba-pum, ba-pum, pa-pum, pa-pum. It was like the sound of a drum beating. The rabbits all around made a big circle and began to dance. They danced and danced. They danced in couples and moved in and out and back and forth. It was a very good dance that the rabbits did. The hunters who were watching found themselves tapping the earth with their hands in the same beat as the big rabbit's foot.

Then, suddenly, the big rabbit stopped thumping the earth. All of the rabbits stopped dancing. BA-BUM! The chief of the rabbits thumped the earth one final time. It leaped high into the air, right over the men's heads, and it was gone. All of the other rabbits ran in every direction out of the clearing and they were gone, too.

The men were astonished at what they had seen. None of them had ever seen anything at all like this. None of them had ever heard or seen such a dance. It was all they could talk about as they went back to the village. All thought of hunting was now gone from their minds.

When they reached the village, they went straight to the longhouse where the head of the Clan Mothers lived. She

It was like the sound of a drum beating.

was a very wise woman and knew a great deal about the animals. They told her their story. She listened closely. When they were done telling the story, she picked up a water drum and handed it to the leader of the hunters.

"Play that rhythm which the Rabbit Chief played," she said.

The leader of the men did as she asked. He played the rhythm of the rabbits' dance.

"That is a good sound," said the Clan Mother. "Now show me the dance which the Rabbit People showed you."

The hunters then did the dance while their leader played the drum. The Clan Mother listened closely and watched. When they were done, she smiled at them.

"I understand what has happened," she said. "The Rabbit People know that we rely on them. We hunt them for food and for clothing. The Rabbit Chief has given us this special dance so that we can honor its people for all that they give to the human beings. If we play their song and do their dance, then they will know we are grateful for all they continue to give us. We must call this new song The Rabbit Dance and we must do it, men and women together, to honor the Rabbit People.

So it was that a new social dance was given to the Iroquois people. To this day the Rabbit Dance is done to thank the Rabbit People for all they have given, not only food and clothing, but also a fine dance that makes the people glad.

It was the clattering of antlers.

The Deer Dance

There was a man who lived in the country far away from any village. He made his living as a hunter, but he always was very respectful of the animals he hunted. This man's name was Walking Man. He always kept his eyes and ears open to everything around him, for he knew how special it was in the wilderness. It was to the wilderness that people went in their dreams, to the place they called Seye Wailo. That name meant many things. It meant the Home of All the Animals. It meant the Home of the Deer. It meant the Place Where Flowers Live. It was said that the best songs always came to people from Seye Wailo.

One day, as Walking Man was out, he heard a sound from a hilltop. It was like a sound he had heard before at the time of year when the deer are mating. It was the clattering of antlers. He knew that the bucks would fight in this way during the mating time, striking their antlers together. But it was not that time of year and this sound was different. It was a softer sound and its rhythm was like that of a song. He went to look, but he could see nothing.

The next morning Walking Man rose before the sun came up and went back to that hilltop. He sat quietly on a

fallen tree and waited as the sun rose. He began to hear that sound again, and he looked carefully. There not far from him were two big deer. They had huge antlers and, as they stood facing each other, they rattled their antlers together. Near them was a young deer. As Walking Man watched, he saw that young deer lift its head and lower it. It ran from side to side, leaping up and down. It seemed happy as it did this. Walking Man knew what he was seeing. He was seeing the deer do their own special dance. Though he had his weapons with him, he did not try to kill them. He watched them dance for a long time.

When Walking Man went down that hill, he had a thought in his mind. There were songs coming into his mind. When he rose the next morning, he went out to walk and as he walked he found a newborn fawn where its mother had left it hidden among the flowers. He made a song for that fawn. Then he went to the village and gathered some of his friends.

"I am going to make songs for the deer," he said.

He took two sticks and put notches on one of them so that he could make the sound of the deer's antlers. He showed one of the boys in the village how the young deer danced and had the boy dance that way as they played the deer song and sang.

So it was that the Deer Dance came to the Yaqui people, a gift from the deer, a gift from Seye Wailo.

He was seeing the deer do their own special dance.

Vision

The eagle
spread its
wings wide.

Eagle Boy

Long ago, a boy was out walking one day when he found a young eagle had fallen from its nest. He picked that eagle up and brought it home and began to care for it. He made a place for it to stay, and each day he went out and hunted for rabbits and other small game to feed it. His mother asked him why he no longer came to work in the fields and help his family. "I must hunt for this eagle," the boy said. So it went on for a long time and the eagle grew large and strong as the boy hunted and fed it. Now it was large enough to fly away if it wished, but it stayed with the boy who had cared for it so well. The boy's brothers criticized him for not doing his part to care for the corn fields and the melon fields, but Eagle Boy did not hear them. He cared only for his bird. Even the boy's father, who was an important man in the village, began to criticize him for not helping. But still the boy did not listen. So it was that the boy's brothers and his older male relatives came together and decided that they must kill the eagle. They decided they would do so when they returned from the fields on the following day.

When Eagle Boy came to his bird's cage, he saw that the bird sat there with its head down. He placed a rabbit he had just caught in the cage, but the eagle did not touch it.

27

"What is wrong, my eagle?" said the boy.

Then the eagle spoke, even though it had never spoken before. "My friend, I cannot eat because I am filled with sorrow," said the eagle.

"Why are you troubled?" said the boy.

"It is because of you," said the eagle. "You have not done your work in the fields. Instead, you have spent all of your time caring for me. Now your brothers and your older male relatives have decided to kill me so that you will again return to your duties in the village. I have stayed here all of this time because I love you. But now I must leave. When the sun rises tomorrow, I will fly away and never come back."

"My eagle," said the boy, "I do not wish to stay here without you. You must take me with you."

"My friend, I cannot take you with me," said the eagle. "You would not be able to find your way through the sky. You would not be able to eat raw food."

"My eagle," said the boy, "I cannot live here without you." So he begged the eagle and at last the great bird agreed.

"If you are certain, then you may come with me. But you must do as I say. Come to me at dawn, after the people have gone down to their fields. Bring food to eat on our long journey across the sky. Put the food in pouches that you can

"Here is my home…"

28

sling over your shoulders. You must also bring two strings
of bells and tie them to my feet."

That night the boy filled pouches with blue corn wafer
bread and dried meat and fruits. He made up two strings of
bells, tying them with strong rawhide. The next morning,
after the people had gone down to the fields, he went to the
eagle's cage and opened it. The eagle spread its wings wide.

"Now," he said to Eagle Boy, "tie the bells to my feet
and then climb onto my back and hold onto the base of my
wings."

Eagle Boy climbed on and the eagle began to fly. It rose
higher and higher in slow circles above the town and above
the field. The bells on the eagle's feet jingled and the eagle
sang and the boy sang with it:

> Huli-i-i, hu-li-i-i
> Pa shish lakwa-a-a-a . . .

So they sang and the people in the fields below heard them
singing, and they heard the sounds of the bells Eagle Boy
had tied to the eagle's feet. They all looked up.

"They are leaving," the people said. "They are leaving."
Eagle Boy's parents called up to him to return, but he could
not hear them. The eagle and the boy rose higher and higher
in the sky until they were only a tiny speck and then they
were gone from the sight of the village people.

The eagle and the boy flew higher and higher until they came to an opening in the clouds. They passed through and came out into the Sky Land. They landed there on Turquoise Mountain where the Eagle People lived. Eagle Boy looked around the sky world. Everything was smooth and white and clean as clouds.

"Here is my home," the eagle said. He took the boy into the city in the sky, and there were eagles all around them. They looked like people, for they took off their wings and their clothing of feathers when they were in their homes.

The Eagle People made a coat of eagle feathers for the boy and taught him to wear it and to fly. It took him a long time to learn, but soon he was able to circle above the land just like the Eagle People and he was an eagle himself.

"You may fly anywhere," the old eagles told him, "anywhere except to the south. Never fly to the South Land."

All went well for Eagle Boy in his new life. One day, though, as he flew alone, he wondered what it was that was so terrible about the south. His curiosity grew, and he flew further and further toward the south. Lower and lower he flew and now he saw a beautiful city below with people dancing around red fires.

"There is nothing to fear here," he said, and flew lower still. Closer and closer he came, drawn by the red fires, until he landed. The people greeted him and drew him into the circle. He danced with them all night and then, when he grew tired,

All went well for Eagle Boy in his new life.

they gave him a place to sleep. When he woke next morning and looked around, he saw that the fires were gone. The houses no longer seemed bright and beautiful. All around him there was dust, and in the dust there were bones. He looked for his cloak of eagle feathers, wanting to fly away from this city of the dead, but it was nowhere to be found. Then the bones rose up and came together. There were people made of bones all around him! He rose and began to run, and the people made of bones chased him. Just as they were about to catch him, he saw a badger.

"Grandson," the badger said, "I will save you." Then the badger carried the boy down into his hole and the bone people could not follow. "You have been foolish," the badger said. "You did not listen to the warnings the eagles gave you. Now that you have been to this land in the south, they will not allow you to live with them anymore."

Then the badger showed Eagle Boy the way back to the city of the eagles. It was a long journey and when the boy reached the eagle city, he stood outside the high white walls. The eagles would not let him enter.

"You have been to the South Land," they said. "You can no longer live with us."

At last the eagle the boy had raised took pity on him. He brought the boy an old and ragged feather cloak.

"With this cloak you may reach the home of your own people," he said. "But you can never return to our place in the sky."

So the boy took the cloak of tattered feathers. His flight back down to his people was a hard one and he almost fell many times. When he landed on the earth in his village, the eagles flew down and carried off his feathered cloak. From then on, Eagle Boy lived among his people. Though he lifted his eyes and watched whenever eagles soared overhead, he shared in the work in the fields, and his people were glad to have him among them.

"But you can never return to our place in the sky."

Feathers
and Fur,
Scales
and Skin

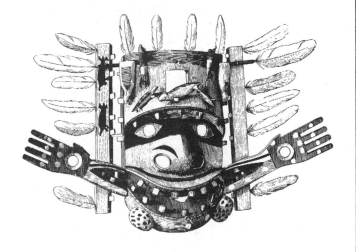

"Who has done this to my pond?" Turtle said.

Turtle Races with Beaver

Long ago, Turtle lived in a small pond. It was a fine place. There were alder trees along the bank to give shade and a fine grassy bank where Turtle could crawl out and sun himself. There were plenty of fish for Turtle to catch. The small pond had everything any turtle could ever want, and Turtle thought his pond was the finest place in the whole world. Turtle spent his time swimming around, sunning himself, and catching fish whenever he was hungry. So it went until the cold winds began to blow down from the north.

"Ah," Turtle said, "It is time for me to go to sleep." Then he dove down to the bottom of the pond and burrowed into the mud. He went to sleep for the winter. He slept so soundly, in fact, that he slept a little later than usual and did not wake up until it was late in the spring. The warming waters of the pond woke him, and he crawled out of the mud and began to swim toward the surface. Something was wrong, though, for it seemed to take much too long to get to the surface of his small pond. Turtle was certain the water had not been that deep when he went to sleep.

As soon as Turtle reached the surface and looked around, he saw that things were not as they should be. His small pond was more than twice its normal size. His fine grassy bank for sunning himself was underwater! His beautiful alder trees had been cut down and made into a big dam.

"Who has done this to my pond?" Turtle said.

Just then Turtle heard a loud sound. WHAP! Turtle turned to look and saw a strange animal swimming toward him across the surface of his pond. It had a big, flat tail and as it came close to Turtle, it lifted up that big, flat tail and hit the surface of the water with it. WHAP!

"Who are you?" Turtle said. "What are you doing in my pond? What have you done to my beautiful trees?"

"Hunh!" the strange animal said. "This is not your pond. This is my pond! I am Beaver and I cut down those trees with my teeth and I built that dam and made this pond nice and deep. This is my pond and you must leave."

"No," Turtle said. "This is my pond. If you do not leave, I will fight you. I am a great warrior."

"Hunh!" Beaver said. "That is good. Let us fight. I will call all my relatives to help me, and they will chew your head off with their strong teeth."

Turtle looked closely at Beaver's teeth. They were long and yellow and looked very sharp.

"What are you
doing in my
pond?"

"Hah!" Turtle said, "I can see it would be too easy to fight you. Instead we should have a contest to decide which of us will leave this pond forever."

"Hunh!" Beaver said. "That is a good idea. Let us see who can stay underwater the longest. I can stay under for a whole day."

As soon as Beaver said that, Turtle saw he would have to think of a different contest. He had been about to suggest that they see who could stay underwater the longest, but if what Beaver said was true, then he would beat Turtle.

"Hah!" Turtle said. "It would be too easy to defeat you that way. Let us have a race instead. The first one to reach the other side of the pond is the winner. The loser must leave my pond forever."

"Hunh!" Beaver said. "That is a good contest. I am the fastest swimmer of all. When I win, you will have to leave my pond forever. Let us begin to race."

"Wait," Turtle said, "I am such a fast swimmer that it would not be fair unless I started from behind you."

Then Turtle placed himself behind Beaver, right next to Beaver's big tail.

"I am ready," Turtle said, "let us begin!"

Beaver began to swim. He was such a fast swimmer that Turtle could barely keep up with him. When they were

halfway across the pond, Turtle began to fall even further behind. But Turtle had a plan. He stuck his long neck out and grabbed Beaver's tail in his jaws.

Beaver felt something grab his tail, but he could not look back. He was too busy swimming, trying to win the race. He swung his tail back and forth, but Turtle held on tight. Now Beaver was almost to the other side of the pond. Turtle bit down even harder. Beaver swung his tail high up into the air, trying to shake free whatever had hold of him. Just as Beaver's tail reached the top of its swing, Turtle let go. He flew through the air and landed on the bank! Beaver looked up, and there was Turtle! Turtle had won the race.

So it was that Beaver had to leave and Turtle, once again, had his pond to himself. With its new deeper waters there were soon even more fish than there had been before and Turtle's alders grew back once more. Truly, Turtle's pond was the finest place in the whole world.

Turtle had won the race.

Octopus and Raven

One morning, as the tide went out, the old people came down to sit and watch by the shore. That was the way it was done in the old days. As they sat there, they saw a woman walking along the beach. Her hair was long and it was strung into eight braids. That woman was Octopus. She carried a basket on her back. There was a yew wood digging stick in her hand. She was going to look for clams. She sat down on one of the stones just at the edge of the water and began to dig. Before long, she dug up one clam and then another.

As the people watched, someone else came along the beach. That person was tall with glossy black hair.

"Look," one of the old people said. "Here comes Raven. He has seen Octopus digging for food. Now he is going to bother her."

"Ah," another of the old people said. "That is not a good idea. You shouldn't bother Octopus!"

Sure enough, just as the old people expected, Raven walked right down to the rock where Octopus sat and began to bother her.

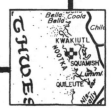

"Are you
digging for
clams?"

"Octopus," Raven said in a loud voice, "what are you doing? Are you digging for clams?"

Octopus didn't answer him or even look up. She just continued to dig with her stick.

Raven stepped a little closer. "Are you digging for clams?" he said, his voice louder still.

Octopus did not look up. She just kept on digging.

Raven came closer. "Are you digging for clams?" he said in an even louder voice.

Octopus didn't answer him. She just kept on digging.

Now Raven came very close indeed. He poked his nose into Octopus' basket. "Are you digging for clams?" he shouted.

Suddenly, Octopus stood up. She dropped her digging stick. Her braids turned into eight long arms. Four of those arms wrapped around Raven and four around the rock.

"Raven," she said, "I am glad you asked me that question. Yes, I am digging clams. It is clams that I am digging."

Raven struggled to get free, but he was caught. The tide had turned now and the water was around his feet. "Octopus," he said, "thank you for answering my question. Now you can let me go."

But Octopus only held him tighter. "Raven," she said, "that is a good question that you asked. Now I must answer you. Yes, I am digging clams. It is clams that I am digging."

The water was growing deeper around them. Now it had reached Raven's knees. He tried to get loose, but Octopus wrapped her arms tighter. "That is a very good answer," Raven said. "I have heard you clearly now. Indeed, you are digging clams. You do a very good job of digging clams. Now please let me go."

But Octopus did not let go. "Raven" she said, "let me answer your question. I am digging clams. It is clams that I am digging."

Now the water was over their waists. Raven saw that it would soon be even deeper. "Octopus," he said, "you do not have to answer me again. It is very clear to me what you were doing. Just let me go now. Please let me go now."

Octopus did not let go. "Raven," she said, "I was digging clams, I was digging clams."

Again Raven begged, but the water continued to get deeper and Octopus held tight. The water came up to their necks and then it was over their heads.

Up on the beach, above the tide line, the old people watched.

"Octopus can hold her breath longer than Raven," one of the old people said.

Her braids turned into eight long arms.

42

They watched and finally, after a long time, Raven
could hold his breath no longer and he drowned. Octopus
let go and Raven floated up to the surface.

"Look," another of the old people said, "Raven has
drowned."

"Don't worry about him," the other old people said.
"He will come back to life again. He always does. His cousin,
Crow, will help."

Then the old people went down and pulled Raven out
of the water. They carried him to his cousin, Crow. Crow
was very wise and she knew just what to do. The next day,
just as the old people said, Raven came back to life again.
But it was a long time before he went back to the shore and
he never asked Octopus another question.

The leaves
would fall from
the trees.

How the Butterflies Came to Be

L ong ago, not long after Earth-Maker shaped the world out of dirt and sweat he scraped from his skin, Iitoi, our Elder Brother, was walking about. It was just after the time of year when the rains come. There were flowers blooming all around him as he walked. The leaves of the trees were green and bright. He came to a village and there he saw the children playing. It made his heart good to see the children happy and playing. Then he became sad. He thought of how those children would grow old and weaken and die. That was the way it was made to be. The red and yellow and white and blue of the flowers would fade. The leaves would fall from the trees. The days would grow short and the nights would be cold.

A wind brushed past Elder Brother, making some fallen yellow leaves dance in the sunlight. Then an idea came to him.

"I will make something," Elder Brother said. "It will make the hearts of the children dance and it will make my own heart glad again."

Then Iitoi took a bag and placed in it the bright-colored flowers and the fallen leaves. He placed many things in that

bag. He placed yellow pollen and white cornmeal and green pine needles in that bag and caught some of the shining gold of the sunlight and placed it in there, as well. There were birds singing around him and he took some of their songs and put them into that bag, too.

"Come here," Elder Brother called to the children, "come here. I have something here for you."

The children came to him and he handed them his bag.

"Open this," he said.

The children opened Elder Brother's bag and out of it flew the first butterflies. Their wings were bright as sunlight and held all of the colors of the flowers and the leaves, the cornmeal, the pollen and the green pine needles. They were red and gold and black and yellow, blue and green and white. They looked like flowers, dancing in the wind. They flew about the heads of the children and the children laughed. As those first butterflies flew, they sang and the children listened.

But as the children listened to the singing butterflies, the songbirds came to Elder Brother.

"Iitoi," the songbirds said, "those songs were given to us. It is fine that you have given these new creatures all the brightest colors, but it is not right that they should also have our songs."

They looked like flowers, dancing in the wind.

46

"Ah," Elder Brother said, "you speak truly. The songs belong to you and not to the butterflies."

So it is to this day. Though they dance as they fly, the butterflies are silent. But still, when the children see them, brightly dancing in the wind, their hearts are glad. That is how Elder Brother meant it to be.

He sank into
the river and
drowned.

Salmon Boy

Long ago, among the Haida people, there was a boy who showed no respect for the salmon. Though the salmon meant life for the people, he was not respectful of the one his people called Swimmer. His parents told him to show gratitude and behave properly, but he did not listen. When fishing he would step on the bodies of the salmon that were caught and after eating he carelessly threw the bones of the fish into the bushes. Others warned him that the spirits of the salmon were not pleased by such behavior, but he did not listen.

One day, his mother served him a meal of salmon. He looked at it with disgust. "This is moldy," he said, though the meat was good. He threw it upon the ground. Then he went down to the river to swim with the other children. However, as he was swimming, a current caught him and pulled him away from the others. It swept him into the deepest water and he could not swim strongly enough to escape from it. He sank into the river and drowned.

There, deep in the river, the Salmon People took him with them. They were returning back to the ocean without

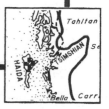

their bodies. They had left their bodies behind for the humans and the animal people to use as food. The boy went with them, for he now belonged to the salmon.

When they reached their home in the ocean, they looked just like human beings. Their village there in the ocean looked much like his own home and he could hear the sound of children playing in the stream which flowed behind the village. Now the Salmon People began to teach him. He was hungry and they told him to go to the stream and catch one of their children, who were salmon swimming in the stream. However, he was told, he must be respectful and after eating return all of the bones and everything he did not intend to eat to the water. Then, he was told, their child would be able to come back to life. But if the bones were not returned to the water, that salmon child could not come back.

He did as he was told, but one day after he had eaten, when it came time for the children to come up to the village from the stream, he heard one of them crying. He went to see what was wrong. The child was limping because one of its feet was gone. Then the boy realized he had not thrown all of the fins back into the stream. He quickly found the one fin he had missed, threw it in and the child was healed.

After he had spent the winter with the Salmon People, it again was spring and time for them to return to the rivers. The boy swam with them, for he belonged to the Salmon People now. When they swam past his village, his own mother caught him in her net. When she pulled him from the water, even though he was in the shape of a salmon, she saw

Now the Salmon People began to teach him.

50

the copper necklace he was wearing. It was the same necklace she had given her son. She carried Salmon Boy carefully
back home. She spoke to him and held him and gradually he
began to shed his salmon skin. First his head emerged. Then,
after eight days, he shed all of the skin and was a human
again.

Salmon Boy taught the people all of the things he had
learned. He was a healer now and helped them when they
were sick.

"I cannot stay with you long," he said, "you must remember what I teach you."

He remained with the people until the time came when
the old salmon who had gone upstream and not been caught
by the humans or the animal people came drifting back
down toward the sea. As Salmon Boy stood by the water, he
saw a huge old salmon floating down toward him. It was so
worn by its journey that he could see through its sides. He
recognized it as his own soul and he thrust his spear into it.
As soon as he did so, he died.

Then the people of the village did as he had told them to
do. They placed his body into the river. It circled four times
and then sank, going back to his home in the ocean, back to
the Salmon People.

*The frogs
would not give
her up.*

The Woman
Who Married a Frog

There once was a young woman who was very proud. She was the daughter of the town chief and her family was very respected. Many of the young men wanted to marry her, but she thought none of them were good enough for her. One day, she was walking with her sister beside the big lake near their village. There were many frogs in that lake. A large number of them were sitting on a mud bank in the middle of the lake and she began to make fun of them.

"How ugly these frogs are," she said. Then she bent over and picked one up which was sitting on the muddy shore and looking up at her. "You are so ugly," she said to the frog. "Even another frog would not want to marry you!" Then she threw the frog back into the lake.

That night, when she stepped outside of her lodge to walk while the others were sleeping, she was surprised to see a young man standing there. His clothing was decorated with green beads and he seemed very handsome.

"I have come to marry you," the young man said. "Come with me to my father's house."

The young woman agreed. She thought she had never seen such a handsome man before and wanted to be his wife.

"We must climb the hill to go to my father's house," the young man said and he pointed toward the lake. They began to walk down toward the water, but it seemed to the young woman they were climbing a hill. When they reached the water they did not stop, but they went under.

The next day, her family noticed that she was missing. They searched for her everywhere and when they found her tracks leading to the water, they decided she had drowned. They beat the drums for a death feast. People cut their hair and blackened their faces and mourned.

One day, though, a man walked down by the lake. When he looked out toward its middle he saw on the mud bank many frogs sitting there. There, in the midst of the frogs, was the chief's missing daughter. He began to wade in toward them, but they leaped into the water, taking the young woman with them.

The man went as quickly as he could to the chief's house. "I have seen your daughter," he said. "She has been taken by the frogs. I tried to reach her, but the Frog People took her with them under the water."

The young woman's father and mother went down to the lake. There they saw their daughter sitting on the mud bank surrounded by the Frog People. As before, when they

"The frogs know our language."

54

tried to reach her, the frogs dove in and carried her under the lake with them. Then the chief's other daughter spoke.

"My sister insulted the frogs," she said, "that is why they have taken her."

The chief saw then what he must do. He made offerings to the Frog People, asking them to forgive his daughter. They placed dishes of food on the surface of the water. The dishes floated out and then sank. But the frogs would not give up the young woman. They placed robes of fine skins on the bank. The young woman and the Frog People came to the bank and took those robes, but when the chief came close, the Frog People drew her back into the lake. The frogs would not give her up. At last the chief made a plan. He gathered together all of the people in the village.

"We will dig a trench," he said. "We will drain away the water of the lake and rescue my daughter."

The people worked for a long time and the water began to drain away. The Frog People tried to fill the trench with mud, but they could not stop the water from flowing out. The frogs tried to drive the people away, but the people only picked the frogs up and dropped them back into the water. They were careful not to hurt any of the frogs, but they did not stop digging the trench. The water continued to flow out and the homes of the Frog People were being destroyed. At last the chief of the frogs decided. It was his son who had married the young woman.

"We are not strong enough to fight these humans," he said. "We must give my new daughter back to her people."

So they brought the young woman to the trench. Her father and mother saw her and they pulled her out. She was covered with mud and smelled like a frog. One frog leaped out of the water after her. It was the frog who had been her husband. But the people carefully picked him up and dropped him back into the lake.

They took the young woman home. For a long time she could only speak as a frog does, "Huh, Huh, Huh!" Finally she learned to speak like a human again.

"The frogs know our language." she told the people. "We must not talk badly about them."

From that day on, her people showed great respect to the frogs. They learned the songs that the woman brought from the Frog People and they used the frog as an emblem. They had learned a great lesson. They never forgot what happened to that young woman who was too proud. To this day, some people in that village still say when they hear the frogs singing in the lake, the frogs are telling their children this story, too.

They had learned a great lesson.

How Poison Came into the World

Back when the world was new, there was a certain plant that grew in the shallow water of the bayous. It grew in the places where the Choctaw people would come to bathe or swim. This vine was very poisonous and whenever the people touched this vine, they would become very sick and die.

This vine liked the Choctaw people and felt sorry for them. It did not want to cause them so much suffering. It could not show itself to them, because it was its nature to grow beneath the surface. So it decided to give its poison away. It called together the chiefs of the small people of the swamps—the bees, wasps and snakes. It told them that it wished to give up its poison.

Those small creatures held council together about the vine's offer. Until then, they had no poison and they were often stepped on by others. They agreed that they would share the poison.

Wasp spoke first. "I will take a small part of your poison," it said. "Then I will be able to defend my nest. But I will

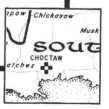

*They agreed
that they would
share the
poison.*

warn the people by buzzing close to them before I poison them. I will keep the poison in my tail."

Bee was next. "I, too, will take a small part of your poison," it said. "I will use it to defend my hive. I will warn the people away before I poison them and even if I should have to use my poison, it will kill me to use it, so I will use it carefully."

Water Moccasin spoke. "I will take some of your poison. I will only use it if people step on me. I will hold it in my mouth and when I open my mouth people will see how white it is and know that they should avoid me."

Last of all, Rattlesnake spoke. "I will take a good measure of your poison," he said. "I will take all that remains. I will hold it in my mouth, too. Before I strike anyone, I will use my tail to warn them. *Intesha, intesha, intesha, intesha.* That is the sound I will make to let them know they are too close."

So it was done. The vine gave up its poison to the bees and wasps, the water moccasin and the rattlesnake. Now the shallow waters of the bayous were safe for the Choctaw people and where once that vine had poison, now it had flowers. From then on, only those who were foolish and did not heed the warnings of the small ones who took the vine's poison were hurt.

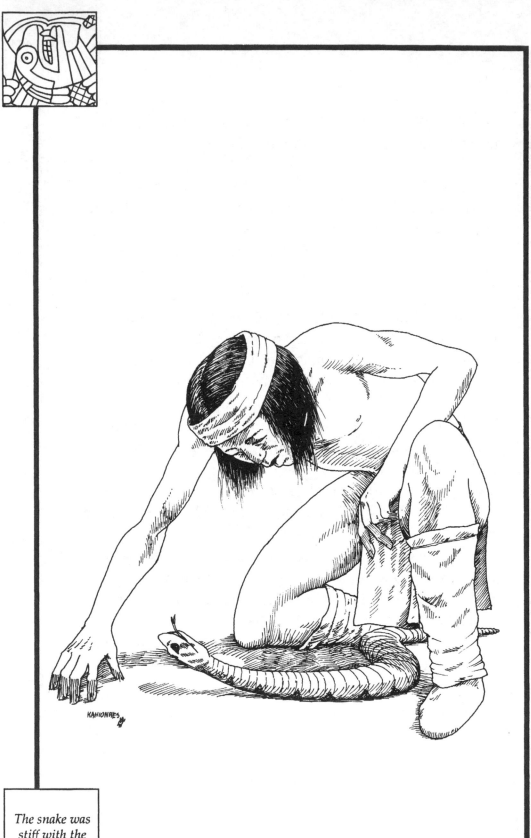

The snake was
stiff with the
cold.

The Boy
and the Rattlesnake

Once there was a boy who was very soft-hearted. One morning, as he was walking along he saw a rattlesnake by the side of the road. There had been an early frost the night before and the snake had been caught out in it. The snake was stiff with the cold. The boy stopped to look at it, feeling sorry for the snake. Then a wonderful thing happened. The snake opened up its mouth and spoke to him.

"Help me," the rattlesnake said in a pitiful voice. "Pick me up, warm me or I will die."

"But if I pick you up, you will bite me," the boy said.

"No," said the snake, "I will not bite you. Pick me up, hold me close to you and warm me or I will die."

So the boy took pity on the snake. He picked it up. He held it close to him so that it would be warmed by his body. The snake grew warmer and less stiff and then, suddenly, it twisted in the boy's hands and—WHAH! It bit the boy on his arm. The boy dropped the snake and grasped his arm.

"Why did you bite me?" the boy said. "You said you would not bite me if I picked you up."

"That is so," said the snake, "but when you picked me up, you knew I was a rattlesnake."

"Help me," the rattlesnake said. "Pick me up, warm me or I will die."

The First Flute

Long ago, it is said, a young man saw a young woman in his village and longed to find some way to talk to her. But he was too shy to approach her directly. She was the daughter of a chief and it was well known that she was very proud. Many men tried to court her, but she sent them all away.

One day, this young man went on a hunting trip. He found the tracks of an elk and began to follow it. Although he caught sight of it now and then, it stayed far ahead of him, leading him away from the village until he was deep in the hills. Finally night came and he made a camp. He was far from home and the sounds in the night made him feel very lonely. He listened to the owls and rustling of the leaves, the creaking of the tree branches and the whistling of the wind. Then he heard a sound he had never heard before. It was a strange sound, like the call of a bird and yet different from any bird. It sounded as if it came from the land of the spirits. Strange as it was, that call was also beautiful. It was like a song and he listened closely to it. Soon he fell asleep and dreamed.

Then he heard a
sound he had
never heard
before.

In his dream, a red-headed woodpecker came and sang that strange and beautiful song. Then the woodpecker spoke. "Follow me," it said. "Follow me and I will give you something. Follow me, follow me."

When the young man woke, the sun was two hands high. There in the branches of the tree above him was the red-headed woodpecker. It began to fly from tree to tree, stopping and looking back. The young man followed. Finally the woodpecker landed on the straight dead branch of a cedar tree. It began drumming with its beak on that hollow limb, which was full of holes made by the woodpecker. Just then a wind came up and blew through the hollow branch. It made the song that the hunter had heard!

Now the hunter saw what he should do. He climbed the tree and carefully broke off that branch. He thanked the red-headed woodpecker for giving him this gift and he took it home to his lodge. But he could not make it sing, no matter what he did. Finally he went to a hilltop and fasted for four days. On the fourth day a vision came to him. It was the woodpecker and it spoke again, telling him what to do. He must carve the likeness of the woodpecker and fasten it in a certain way near one end of the branch. He must shape the other end of the flute so it looked like the head and open mouth of a bird. Then when he blew into that end of the flute and covered the holes with his fingers, he would be able to play that song.

The man did as his vision told him. He carved the flute so that it looked like the head and open mouth of a bird. He

tied on the bird reed near the other end and when he blew into the flute it made music. Then he began to practice long and hard, listening to the sounds of the wind and the trees, the rippling of the waters and the calls of the birds, making them all part of his playing. Soon he was able to play a beautiful song. Now when he hunted and camped far from the village he had his flute with him and could play it to keep himself company.

Finally, he knew that he was ready to visit that young woman he had liked so long from afar. He went and stood behind her lodge and played his best song on the flute. She heard that song and came out into the moonlight. She went straight to where he was playing. She walked up to him and stood close to him and he lifted his blanket and wrapped it around them both.

So it was that the young hunter became the husband of the chief's daughter. He became a great man among his people. Ever since then, young men who wish to go courting have learned to make the cedar flute and play those magical songs. And many of those flutes, to give honor to the red-headed woodpecker that gave such a special gift, have been shaped like the head and open mouth of a bird.

Soon he was able to play a beautiful song.

Manabozho
and the Woodpecker

Manabozho lived with his grandmother, Nokomis, in their lodge near the big water. As Manabozho grew older, his grandmother taught him many things. One day she told him about Megissogwon, the Spirit of Fever.

"Megissogwon is very strong," she told him. "He is the one who killed your grandfather."

When Manabozho learned about Megissogwon he decided that he should destroy him. "Things will be hard for the people to come," Manabozho said. "I will go and kill this monster."

Nokomis warned her grandson that it would not be easy to do. The way to Megissogwon's island was a dangerous one. It was guarded by two great serpents that waited on either side and breathed fire on anyone who tried to pass through. If one got past them, the waters of the lake turned into black mud and pitch that would stop the passage of any canoe. However, Manabozho was determined.

"Grandmother," he said, "I must go and fight Megissogwon."

*Manabozho shot
his arrows at
Megissogwon.*

Then Manabozho fasted and prayed for four days. He loaded his birchbark canoe with many arrows. He took with him a bag made from the bladder of the sturgeon which was filled with fish oil. He spoke a single word to his canoe and it shot forward across the water. It went so swiftly that he was soon to the place where the lake narrowed and the two great snakes waited on either side.

"Manabozho," the great snakes said, "if you pass between us we shall destroy you with our fire."

"That is true," Manabozho said. "I can see that your power is stronger than mine. But what about that other one there behind you?"

The two great serpents turned their heads to look behind them. As soon as they did so Manabozho spoke another word to his canoe and it shot between the two great serpents. He lifted his bow and fired his flint-tipped arrows, killing both of the serpents. Then he went on his way.

Now he came to the place where the waters turned into black mud and pitch. He took out the fish bladder and poured the slippery fish oil all over the sides of his canoe. Then he spoke another word and his canoe shot forward, sliding through the mud and pitch.

At last Manabozho came to the island of Megissogwon. Only a single tree still stood on the island, for Megissogwon hated the birds and had destroyed all the other trees to keep

them away. On that tree there was a single branch and on it sat Woodpecker.

"My friend," Manabozho said to Woodpecker, "I am glad to see you. I have come to destroy that one who hates us."

Then Manabozho called out in a loud voice as if speaking to many men. "My warriors," he said, "surround this island. I shall fight the monster first, but be ready to attack when I call for help."

Megissogwon heard Manabozho's voice and came running to attack him. He was taller than any man and his face and his hands were painted black. His hair was bound up tightly in a knot on top of his head. His body was covered with wampum painted in bright stripes. He roared as he came and his voice was so loud that it shook the ground.

"You are the one who killed my grandfather," Manabozho shouted. "My men and I will destroy you."

Then they began to fight. Manabozho shot his arrows at Megissogwon. The monster had no weapons, but his breath was colder than winter ice and he tried to grasp Manabozho with his black hands. Each time he came close, though, Manabozho would shout out as if to other warriors. "Now, attack him from behind."

Whenever Manabozho shouted, Megissogwon would turn to look. Thus Manabozho would escape his grasp and shoot another arrow at the monster. But Megissogwon's

Manabozho called Woodpecker to him.

armor of wampum was so strong that the arrows just bounced off.

So they fought all through the day. Now the sun was about to set and Manabozho had only three arrows left.

Then Woodpecker called down to Manabozho from the place where he sat on that one last tree.

"Shoot at the top of his head," Woodpecker called, "his power is there, wrapped up in the knot of his hair."

Megissogwon was reaching for Manabozho with his huge black hands. His breath was cold on Manabozho's face. Manabozho took careful aim and shot. His arrow grazed the giant's hair and Megissogwon staggered.

"Shoot again, shoot again!" Woodpecker called.

Manabozho shot his second arrow. It struck Megissogwon's topknot and the giant fell to his knees.

"Shoot again, shoot again!" Woodpecker cried.

Manabozho aimed at the center of the giant's knot of hair. His arrow flew straight to its mark and Megissogwon fell dead.

Manabozho called Woodpecker to him.

"My friend," he said, "this victory is also yours."

Then he took some of the giant's blood and placed it on Woodpecker's crest, making its head red. To this day, Woodpecker has a red head, reminding everyone of how it helped Manabozho defeat the Spirit of Fever, reminding the people to always respect the birds.

To this day, Woodpecker has a red head.

Why Coyote Has Yellow Eyes

Coyote Woman lived near Skeleton Man. Skeleton Man lived near Coyote Woman. That is how it was. One day, as Coyote Woman was walking around, looking for food, she passed by Skeleton Man's place. Skeleton Man was sitting and doing something very strange. Coyote Woman stopped to watch him.

What Skeleton Man was doing was this. He would sing a certain song. "Hiii aya, hiiiyahahey!" Then his eyes would fly right out of his head. They would fly toward the south until they were out of sight. Then, as Coyote Woman watched, Skeleton Man's eyes came flying back and went right back into his head again!

"Ah," Skeleton Man said, "I have seen so many things."

Coyote Woman walked up to him. "I like that song you were singing," she said.

"Hep owiy!" Skeleton Man said. "Yes. It is a good song. When I sing it I see things I have not seen before. I saw a

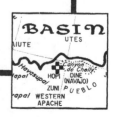

"Hep owiy!"
Skeleton Man
said.

canyon and it was just filled with game animals. Deer and rabbits were there and all kinds of other animals."

Coyote Woman thought about all those game animals. "Will you teach me to sing that song also?" Coyote Woman said.

"It is easy," Skeleton Man said. "Just face to the south and sing like this." Then he sang again, "Hiii aya, hiiiyahahey." As he sang, his eyes flew out toward the south. He sat there and waited and before too long, his eyes came back again.

"That is easy," Coyote Woman said, "I can do that, too."

"Just be sure to face to the south and do not move," Skeleton Man said. Then he disappeared.

"I will see that canyon," Coyote Woman said. She sat down and faced south and she sang very hard. "Hiii aya hiiiyahahey." Her eyes came out of her head and flew toward the south. "Hep owiy!" Coyote Woman said, "I can see the game animals. This canyon is a good place." She got so excited that she began to move around. Soon she was facing toward the north.

"Now," Coyote Woman said, "it is time for my eyes to come back. Come back to me, eyes!" But her eyes did not come back. She called them again, but nothing happened. She called four times and now she could no longer see anything. "Is ohi!" she said. "What am I going to do? I can no longer see anything. Where are my eyes? I called them back to me."

Then Coyote Woman had an idea. She didn't realize that she was no longer facing south and that her eyes could not return to her because she was facing the wrong way. "I know what has happened," she said. "My eyes came back to me but they missed my head. They are on the ground here near me. I have to look for them."

Coyote Woman began to feel around for her lost eyes. She looked and looked and finally found something just the shape of one of her eyes on the end of a stalk. "Here is one of them," she said. Then she found another round thing which felt like an eye on the end of another stalk. "Here is the other one," she said. She lifted them up and popped them into her eye sockets. Now she could see, but everything looked yellow.

"Huih," she said, "my eyes are not working so well. They were outside of my head too long. I had better go find my children."

Then Coyote Woman trotted home. But as soon as her children saw her, they were afraid. Her eyes were big and yellow and frightened them. They ran in all directions to get away from her.

Coyote Woman chased her children, "Come back," she called. But they continued to run away. Coyote Woman had put two big gourds in her head for eyes and now her eyes were big and yellow and frightening. So it has been ever since then that all coyotes have yellow eyes and coyotes live scattered all over the place. And here is where this story has an end.

"Where are my eyes?"

The Dogs Who
Saved Their Master

There was a man who always treated his dogs well. He
fed them good food and spoke kindly to them. He
petted them and allowed them into his lodge. His four dogs
were all great hunters, but the best of all was the smallest
one. It had two black spots on its head, one over each eye.
This dog he called Four Eyes.

One day, as the man was out hunting with his dogs in a
place far to the north where he had never been before, he
found a strange animal trail. Though his dogs whined and
tried to draw him away, he began to follow that trail. Deeper
into the thick forest he went. He saw how the branches on
either side of the trail were broken as if some large animal
had passed along this way.

At last he came to a clearing. There stood a giant dead
tree broken off at its top. The dogs growled and the man
looked up. There, crawling out of the hollow in the tree was
a terrible animal. The man could not move at first, for it was
looking right at him, but the four dogs pushed against the
hunter. They turned him around and he was able to run.
From behind him he heard the sound of a battle as his four

The monster is
closer now.

dogs fought with the terrible animal. He turned back to help
them, but the little white dog with the two black spots on its
head blocked his way.

"My friend," the dog said, "you must run. My brothers
and I will try to hold the monster."

The hunter was surprised. His dog had never spoken
before. But he did as he was told. He ran as fast as he could,
following the trail south. He ran until he could run no longer.
Just as he stopped, the yelp of a dog came from the north
followed by a terrible howl. He knew that one of his dogs
had died. The hunter knelt, trying to regain his strength. His
little white dog came out of the bushes.

"My friend," Four Eyes said, "the monster has killed my
brother, Bear Killer. Now you must run. We will try to hold
it here."

The man rose to his feet and began to run again as Four
Eyes bounded back up the trail. Again he heard the sound of
fighting close behind him and he ran without stopping. He
ran and ran until once more he heard the dying yelp of a dog
followed by that terrible howl. The hunter fell to the ground,
filled with despair. The little white dog came from the bushes
and nudged him.

"My friend," Four Eyes said, "my brother Long Tooth is
dead. The monster is closer now. You must run or our sacrifice will mean nothing."

The hunter forced himself to rise and the little white dog ran back up the trail. Stumbling as he ran, the man heard the sound of fighting close behind. He had only run for a short time when again he heard the yelp of a dog and the monster's howl. The hunter fell to his face. He had no strength to run further. He felt something licking his feet and turned his head to see his small white dog.

"My friend," Four Eyes said, "by licking your feet I have given you new strength to run. You have seen my brothers and me doing this in the past. It is part of our medicine. Now you must go. My brother, Holds Fast, is dead. I shall do my best to stop the monster. But before you go, if you escape, I must ask two favors of you."

The man looked at his little white dog. Its body was covered with wounds. Tears filled his eyes as he nodded his head.

"Ask anything," the hunter said, "and I shall try to do it."

"If you escape," Four Eyes said, "come back and gather our bones to give us proper burial. As a second favor, I ask that you take care of my wife. You may not know her, but the man who thinks of himself as her master does not feed her much and strikes her often. He is the heavy-footed one who does not know how to hunt. If you care for my wife, you may see my brothers and me again. Now, run fast. The monster is close."

The man leaped to his feet and ran. It was as if he had wings. Never had he run so swiftly before. He sped along

"Now, run fast. The monster is close."

the trail and as he ran he saw familiar landmarks. With his
new speed he had traveled far. The sun now was near the
western edge of the sky. His village was close. He had heard
no sound of pursuit or battle behind him. He began to hope
that he would escape.

Suddenly, from right behind him, came the terrible
howl. His legs weakened. He felt the monster's hot breath on
the back of his neck. But just as he began to fall, out from the
bushes in front of him leaped his little white dog. It went
straight for the monster's throat. The man rose and staggered on as the sound of the battle continued behind him. It
was dark now, but he knew the path.

Ahead of him were lights, the fires of his village. Just as
he reached its edge, a terrible cry split the air, louder than
any of the howls before. Then all was silent.

The people of the village came out, frightened by that
cry. The man fell down among them. When he woke the next
morning, he led a party of men back along the trail. Not far
from the village, they found the body of the little white dog.
In Four Eyes' teeth was a great piece of skin torn from the
monster. It was like no skin anyone had ever seen before. A
great trail of blood led back toward the north. The hunter
and the other men followed it. After a day's journey, they
found the bones of Holds Fast. After another day's journey,
they found the bones of Long Tooth and after another day
those of Bear Killer. The blood trail continued on to the
north, but they did not follow it.

The hunter brought the bones of his faithful dogs back home and buried them. He went to the lodge of Heavy Foot.

"I will trade you this old bear skin for your dog," the hunter said.

Heavy Foot thought at first to refuse. Then he saw the look in the hunter's eyes and he quickly agreed. His little white dog had never led him to any game anyway. She was no good as a hunter.

The hunter took the wife of Four Eyes home. He fed her well and cared for her. He saw that she was expecting and he began to understand the promise Four Eyes had made. When the four pups were born, one of them was a little white dog with two black spots over its eyes. When its eyes opened, they looked up at the hunter in a knowing way.

With his new speed he had traveled far.

Why Possum
Has a Naked Tail

In the old days, Possum had the most beautiful tail of all the animals. It was covered with long silky hair and Possum liked nothing better than to wave it around when the Animal People met together in council. He would hold up his tail and show it to the Animal People.

"You see my tail," he would say. "Is it not the most beautiful tail you have ever seen? Surely it is finer than any other animal's!"

He was so proud of his tail that the other animals became tired of hearing him brag about it. Finally, Rabbit decided to do something about it. Rabbit was the messenger for the animals and he was the one who always told them when there was to be a council meeting. He went to Possum's house.

"My friend," Rabbit said, "there is going to be a great meeting. Our chief, Bear, wants you to sit next to him in council. He wants you to be the first one to speak because you have such a beautiful tail."

KAHIONHES

Possum did as
Rabbit said.

Possum was flattered. "It is true," he said, "one who has such a beautiful and perfect tail as I have should be the first one to speak in council." He held up his tail, combing it with his long fingers. "Is not my tail the most wonderful thing you have ever seen?"

Rabbit looked close at Possum's tail.

"My friend," Rabbit said, "it seems to me as if your tail is just a little dirty. I think that it would look even better if you would allow me to clean it. I have some special medicine that will make your tail look just the way it should look."

Possum looked close at his tail. It did seem as if it was a little bit dirty. "Yes," Possum said, "that is a good idea. I want all of the animals to admire my tail when I speak in council."

Then Rabbit mixed up his medicine. It was very strong, so strong that it loosened all of the hair on Possum's tail. But as he put the medicine on Possum's tail he wrapped the tail in the skin which had been shed by a snake.

"This snakeskin will make sure the medicine works well," Rabbit said. "Do not take it off until you speak in council tomorrow. Then the people will all see your tail just as it should be seen."

Possum did as Rabbit said. He kept the snakeskin wrapped tightly around his tail all through the night.

The next day, when the animals met for council, Possum sat next to Chief Bear. As soon as the meeting began, he stood up to speak. As he spoke, he walked back and forth, swinging his tail, which was wrapped in the snakeskin. He smiled as he thought of how good his tail would look because of the medicine Rabbit put on it. All of the animals were watching him very closely, looking at his tail. Possum grinned at the thought of how beautiful his tail would look. The time was right.

"My friends," Possum said, holding up his tail and beginning to unwrap the snakeskin, "I have been chosen to start this council because of my tail. It is the finest of all the tails. Look at my beautiful tail!"

Possum pulled off the snakeskin wrapping and as he did so, all of the hair fell off his tail. His tail was naked and ugly and when Possum saw it, the grin froze on his face. All of the animals were looking at him. Possum was so ashamed, that he fell down on the ground and pretended to be dead. He did not move until long after all the other animals had gone.

To this day, Possum still has that foolish grin on his face and whenever he feels threatened, he pretends that he is dead. And, because he was so vain, Possum has the ugliest tail of all the animals.

"It is the finest of all the tails."

Survival

It is much easier now for them to survive.

How the Fawn Got Its Spots

Long ago, when the world was new, Wakan Tanka, The Great Mystery, was walking around. As he walked, he spoke to himself of the many things he had done to help the four-legged ones and the birds survive.

"It is good," Wakan Tanka said. "I have given Mountain Lion sharp claws and Grizzly Bear great strength. It is much easier now for them to survive. I have given Wolf sharp teeth and I have given his little brother, Coyote, quick wits. It is much easier now for them to survive. I have given Beaver a flat tail and webbed feet to swim beneath the water and teeth which can cut down the trees and I have given slow-moving Porcupine quills to protect itself. Now it is easier for them to survive. I have given the birds their feathers and the ability to fly so that they may escape their enemies. I have given speed to the deer and the rabbit so that it will be hard for their enemies to catch them. Truly it is now much easier for them to survive."

However, as Wakan Tanka spoke, a mother deer came up to him. Behind her was her small fawn, wobbling on weak new legs.

"Great One," she said. "It is true that you have given many gifts to the four-leggeds and the winged ones to help them survive. It is true that you gave me great speed and now my enemies find it hard to catch me. My speed is a great protection, indeed. But what of my little one here? She does not yet have speed. It is easy for our enemies, with their sharp teeth and their claws, to catch her. If my children do not survive, how can my people live?"

"Wica yaka pelo!" said Wakan Tanka. "You have spoken truly; you are right. Have your little one come here and I will help her."

Then Wakan Tanka made paint from the earth and the plants. He painted spots upon the fawn's body so that, when she lay still, her color blended in with the earth and she could not be seen. Then Wakan Tanka breathed upon her, taking away her scent.

"Now," Wakan Tanka said, "your little ones will always be safe if they only remain still when they are away from your side. None of your enemies will see your little ones or be able to catch their scent."

So it has been from that day on. When a young deer is too small and weak to run swiftly, it is covered with spots that blend in with the earth. It has no scent and it remains very still and close to the earth when its mother is not by its side. And when it has grown enough to have the speed Wakan Tanka gave its people, then it loses those spots it once needed to survive.

My speed is a great protection, indeed.

90

The Alligator and the Hunter

There once was a man who had very bad luck when he hunted. Although the other hunters in his village were always able to bring home deer, this man never succeeded. He was the strongest of the men in the village and he knew the forest well, but his luck was never good. Each time he came close to the deer, something bad would happen. A jay would call from the trees and the deer would take flight. He would step on dry leaves and the deer would run before he could shoot. His arrow would glance off a twig and miss the deer. It seemed there was no end to his troubles. Finally the man decided he would go deep into the swamps where there were many deer. He would continue hunting until he either succeeded or lost his own life.

The man hunted for three days without success. At noon on the fourth day, he came to a place in the swamp where there had once been a deep pool. The late summer had been a very dry one, however, and now there was only hot sand where once there had been water. There, resting on the sand, was a huge alligator. It had been without water for many days. It was so dry and weak that it was almost dead. Although the hunter's own luck had been bad, he saw that this alligator's luck was even worse.

"Come close so I can talk to you."

"My brother," said the man, "I pity you."

Then the alligator spoke. Its voice was so weak that the man could barely hear it. "Is there water nearby?" said the alligator.

"Yes," said the man. "There is a deep pool of clear cool water not far from here. It is just beyond that small stand of trees to the west. There the springs never dry up and the water always runs. If you go to that place, you will survive."

"I cannot travel there by myself," said the alligator. "I am too weak. Come close so I can talk to you. I will not harm you. Help me and I will also help you."

The hunter was afraid of the great alligator, but he came a bit closer. As soon as he was close, the alligator spoke again.

"I know that you are a hunter but the deer always escape from you. If you help me, I will make you a great hunter. I will give you the power to kill many deer."

This sounded good to the hunter, but he still feared the alligator's great jaws. "My brother," the man said, "I believe that you will help me, but you are still an alligator. I will carry you to that place, but you must allow me to bind your legs and bind your jaws so that you can do me no harm."

Immediately the alligator rolled over to its back and held up its legs. "Do as you wish," the alligator said.

The man bound the alligator's jaws firmly with his sash. He made a bark strap and bound the alligator's legs together. Then, with his great strength, he lifted the big alligator to his shoulders and carried it to the deep cool water where the springs never dried. He placed the alligator on its back close to the water and he untied its feet. He untied the alligator's jaws, but still held those jaws together with one hand. Then he jumped back quickly. The alligator rolled into the pool and dove underwater. It stayed under a long time and then came up. Three more times the alligator dove, staying down longer each time. At last it came to the surface and floated there, looking up at the hunter who was seated high on the bank.

"You have done as you said you would," said the alligator. "You have saved me. Now I shall help you, also. Listen closely to me now and you will become a great hunter. Go now into the woods with your bow and arrows. Soon you will meet a small doe. That doe has not yet grown large enough to have young ones. Do not kill that deer. Only greet it and then continue on and your power as a hunter will increase. Soon after that you will meet a large doe. That doe has fawns and will continue to have young ones each year. Do not kill that deer. Greet it and continue on and you will be an even greater hunter. Next you will meet a small buck. That buck will father many young ones. Do not kill it. Greet it and continue on and your power as a hunter will become greater still. At last you will meet an old buck, larger than any of the others. Its time on Earth has been useful. Now it is ready to give itself to you. Go close to that deer and shoot it. Then greet it and thank it for giving itself to you. Do this and you will be the greatest of hunters."

"Help me and I will also help you."

94

The hunter did as the alligator said. He went into the forest and met the deer, killing only the old buck. He became the greatest of the hunters in his village. He told this story to his people. Many of them understood the alligator's wisdom and hunted in that way. That is why the Choctaws became great hunters of the deer. As long as they remembered to follow the alligator's teachings, they were never hungry.

KANIRTAKERON

Then the
Great Spirit
made the
Inupiaq.

The Gift of the Whale

When the Great Spirit created this land, he made many beautiful and good things. He made the sun and moon and stars. He made the wide land, white with snow, and the mountains and the ocean. He made fish of all kinds and the many birds. He made the seals and the walrus and the great bears. Then the Great Spirit made the Inupiaq. He had a special love for the people and showed them how to live, using everything around them.

Then, after making all this, the Great Spirit decided to make one thing more. This would be the best creation of all. The Great Spirit made this being with great care. It was the Bowhead Whale. It was, indeed, the most beautiful and the finest of the things made by the Great Spirit. As it swam, it flowed through the ocean. It sang as it went, and it was in perfect balance with everything around it.

But the Great Spirit saw something else. He saw that the Inupiaq people needed the Bowhead Whale. Without the whale, it would be hard for them to survive. They needed to eat muktuk, the flesh of the whale, to keep warm and healthy during the long, cold nights. They needed its bones to help

build their homes. They needed every part of the great whale.

So the Great Spirit gave the Bowhead to the Inupiaq. He gave them a way to hunt it from their boats covered with walrus hide. He made a special time each spring, when the ice of the ocean would break apart to form a road where the whales would swim. In that whale road, the Open Lead, the whales would come to the surface and wait there to be struck by the harpoons of the Inupiaq. They would continue to do so every year as long as the Inupiaq showed respect to the Bowhead, as long as the Inupiaq only took the few whales that they needed in order to survive.

But the Great Spirit decided this also. At that time each year when the Open Lead formed, when the whales came to the surface to be hunted, the Great Spirit made it so that a heavy cloud of thick mist would hang just above the ice, just above the heads of the whales and the Inupiaq. That thick mist would hang there between the sea and the sky. "Though I give you permission to kill my most perfect creation," the Great Spirit said, "I do not wish to watch it."

They needed every part of the great whale.

The Passing of the Buffalo

Once, not long ago, the buffalo were everywhere. Wherever the people were, there were the buffalo. They loved the people and the people loved the buffalo. When the people killed a buffalo, they did it with reverence. They gave thanks to the buffalo's spirit. They used every part of the buffalo they killed. The meat was their food. The skins were used for clothing and to cover their tipis. The hair stuffed their pillows and saddlebags. The sinews became their bowstrings. From the hooves they made glue. They carried water in the bladders and stomachs. To give the buffalo honor, they painted the skull and placed it facing the rising sun.

Then the whites came. They were new people, as beautiful and as deadly as the black spider. The whites took the lands of the people. They built the railroad to cut the lands of the people in half. It made life hard for the people and so the buffalo fought the railroad. The buffalo tore up the railroad tracks. They chased away the cattle of the whites. The buffalo loved the people and tried to protect their way of life. So the army was sent to kill the buffalo. But even the soldiers could not hold the buffalo back. Then the army

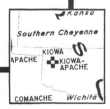

The whites took
the lands of the
people.

hired hunters. The hunters came and killed and killed. Soon
the bones of the buffalo covered the land to the height of a
tall man. The buffalo saw they could fight no longer.

One morning, a Kiowa woman whose family was running from the Army rose early from their camp deep in the
hills. She went down to the spring near the mountainside to
get water. She went quietly, alert for enemies. The morning
mist was thick, but as she bent to fill her bucket she saw
something. It was something moving in the mist. As she
watched, the mist parted and out of it came an old buffalo
cow. It was one of the old buffalo women who always led
the herds. Behind her came the last few young buffalo warriors,
their horns scarred from fighting, some of them wounded.
Among them were a few calves and young cows.

Straight toward the side of the mountain, the old buffalo
cow led that last herd. As the Kiowa woman watched, the
mountain opened up in front of them and the buffalo walked
into the mountain. Within the mountain the earth was green
and new. The sun shone and the meadowlarks were singing.
It was as it had been before the whites came. Then the mountain closed behind them. The buffalo were gone.

Afterword

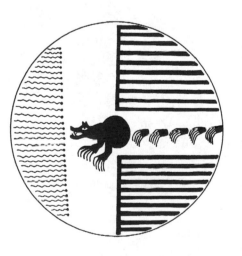

Some men say
they have
been near that
place.

The Lake of the Wounded

Deep within the Smoky Mountains, the Aniyunwiya people say, west of the headwaters of the Ocanaluftee River, there is a lake called Ataga'hi. No hunter has ever seen this lake, for it is the place the animals go to heal themselves when they are wounded. Some men say they have been near that place. As they walked through the mists across what seemed to be a barren flat, they began to hear the wings of water birds and the sound of water falling. But they could not find Ataga'hi.

Some of those who have lived as friends of the animals have been granted a vision of the lake. After praying and fasting all through the night, they have seen the springs flowing down from the high cliffs of the mountains into the stream that feeds Ataga'hi. Then, just at dawn, they have caught a glimpse of wide purple waters and the birds and the animals bathing in those waters and growing well again. But as soon as they have seen it, that vision has faded away, for the animals keep the lake invisible to all hunters.

It is said that there are bear tracks everywhere around Ataga'hi, for the bear is a great healer. One of those who saw

Ataga'hi in the old days said that she saw a wounded bear with a great spear wound in its side plunge into the purple water and come out whole and strong on the other shore.

It is hard today to see Ataga'hi, and some think that its sacred waters have dried. But it is still there, the Cherokee say, hidden deep in the mountains and guarded by the animals. If you treat all the animals with respect, live well and pray, it may be that some day you will see the purple waters of Ataga'hi, too.

It is said that there are bear tracks everywhere around...

Glossary and
Pronunciation Key

The following rules are used for the phonetic description of how each word is pronounced:
1. A line appears over long vowels. Short vowels are unmarked. For instance, "date" would appear as dāt, while "bat" would appear as bat.
2. An accent mark (ʹ) shows which syllable in each word or name is the one emphasized.
3. Syllables are broken with a hyphen (-).
4. Syllables are spelled out as they are pronounced. For instance, "Cherokee" appears as "chair-oh-key."

Where appropriate, the culture from which each word or name comes is given in brackets [ ], followed by the meaning of that word or name, or an explanation of its significance as it appears in the text.

Abenaki (Abʹ-er-na-kee or Abʹ-eh-na-kee). People living at the sunrise, "People of the Dawn." A northeastern Algonquian group.

Achumawi (Ah-shooʹ-mah-wee). The name *Achumawi* means "River People." The Achumawi or Pit River Indian people's homeland is the area of northern California between Mount Shasta and Mount Lassen on one side and the Warner Range on the other.

adobe (ah-dōʹ-bey). [Spanish, from Arabic *atobe*] Sun dried bricks.

Akwesasne (Ah-kwey-sahsʹ-nēē). Literally "where the partridge drums." The Mohawk name for their community along the St. Lawrence River in northern New York and southern Quebec and Ontario.

Aleut (Alʹ-ēē-ūt). *See* Aleutian Islands.

Aleutian Islands (Ah-lūʹ-shun). A string of islands stretching from the southwest tip of Alaska almost to the coast of Siberia. "Aleut" is the name the Russians gave to the people of these islands. They call themselves *Unangan*, literally "Those of the Seaside." They are related to the Inuit-Inupiaq people (Eskimo).

Algonquian (Al-gonʹ-kee-en). Large diverse grouping of native peoples related by a common linguistic root. Algonquian Indians live in the Atlantic coastal regions from what we now call the Maritime Provinces of Canada to the southeastern United States, west to the Prairie Provinces and down through the central states into Wyoming and Montana.

all my relations. Words spoken when entering or leaving a sweat lodge. A translation of the Lakota Sioux words *Mitakuye oyasin* (Mē-tah´-koo-yeh oh-yah´-seen).

American Indian. Term used to refer to the native aboriginal inhabitants of North, Central and South America. Used interchangeably with the newer term "Native American" in the United States. In Canada, the terms "Native," "Indian," "Métis" or "Aboriginal" are commonly used rather than "Native American." In most cases in this book, we have used "Native North American" to refer to the native peoples of the United States and Canada. In all cases, it is best to refer first to the person with regard to the individual tribal nation—for example, "Lakota" or "Abenaki" or "Dine." *See* Native American.

Anishinabe (Ah-nish-ih-nah´-bey) or Anishinabeg. The native people found in the central and northern Great Lakes areas of North America. They are the same people known as the Ojibway and the Chippewa, names applied to them in the last few centuries and used widely today by Anishinabe people themselves. *Ojibway* (O-jib´-wah) was a name given them by their neighbors and probably means "Those Who Make Pictographs." *Anishinabe* means "First Men" or "Original Men." *Chippewa* is a variant of Ojibway. (Ojibway is also translated as "puckered up," referring to their moccasin style which is puckered in front.) Currently the Anishinabe are one of the largest native groups, with a U.S. and Canadian population of over 160,000.

Apache (Ah-patch´-ē). [Zuni Pueblo *Ahpachu*, meaning "The Enemy"] Word used commonly today to refer to the people who call themselves *Tineh* (Tih-ney)—"The People."

Ataga´hi (Ah-tah-gah´-hee). [Cherokee] "The Lake of the Wounded."

Azaban (Ahz-bahn´). Abenaki word for "raccoon," referring both to the animal itself and the trickster hero of Abenaki lesson stories.

Bear Clan. One of the three main clans of the Haudenosaunee (Iroquois) people—Turtle, Bear and Wolf—that are found among all five original Iroquois nations. Clan is inherited from the mother.

Black Elk (1863–1950). A Lakota (Sioux) visionary and medicine man of the late nineteenth and early twentieth century. The story of his life, as recorded by John Neihardt, *Black Elk Speaks: Being the Life Story of a Holy Man of the Oglala Sioux*, is regarded as a minor classic of American literature. The words of this *wichasha wakan* (holy man) are also recorded in *The Sacred Pipe* by Joseph Epes Brown and in *The Sixth Grandfather*, edited by Raymond J. DeMaille.

Cayuga (Kah´-yū-gah). [Iroquois] One of the six nations of the Iroquois confederacy, "People of the Swampy Land."

Cherokee (Chair-oh-kēy´). Corruption of a Lenni Lenape [Delaware] Indian name (*Talligewi* or *Tsa la gi*) for this very large southeastern tribe who

called themselves *Ani Yunwiya* (Ah-nee Yuhn-wi-yah)—"Real People."
One of the so-called (by whites) "Five Civilized Tribes."

chief. This is one of the most widely used and misunderstood words applied to
native people today. All too often, every Indian man is called "Chief" by
non-Indians. In some cases, this can be seen as an insult, especially if that
man is *not* a chief. Other native men, who, indeed, are "chiefs" do not mind
having that word applied to them. Early Europeans thought a "chief"
among the native people of the Americas was like a king, and they even
called many traditional leaders "king" (e.g., King Philip, who was known
as Metacomet by his own *Wampanoag* (Wom-pah-nō´-ag) people. In
general, a chief was a person chosen by his people to lead them. He was
not all-powerful and the roles of such "chiefs" varied widely from one part
of North America to another. In many tribal nations, if a chief did not
behave properly, he was taken out of office by the people. Sitting Bull once
explained that a chief, by definition, has to be a poor man because he must
share everything he has. "Chief," therefore, is not a term to be used lightly.

Chief Seattle (1786?–1866). Seattle, sometimes called Sealth, was a leader of the
Duwamish League of Puget Sound and a strong American ally during the
wars between the United States and a number of northwestern native
nations between 1855 and 1860. The present-day city of Seattle, Washington, bears his name. He is best remembered for a speech ascribed to him
that sets out eloquently the relation between human beings and the natural
world.

Chippewa (Chip´-ah-wah). *See* Anishinabe.

Choctaw (Chock´-taw). A people of Mississippi and Alabama. One of the so-
called "Five Civilized Tribes."

circle. The circle is seen as a special symbol for many native people. It is continu-
ous and all-embracing. When people gather and form a circle, the circle can
always be made larger to include more. Those who sit on the circle are all
at the same height, and all are the same distance from the center—thus it
promotes and stands for equality. The "Sacred Hoop" referred to by many
of the native people of the Plains is another vision of the circle and stands
for life itself, continuing, never-ending, as well as standing for "the
nation."

clan. Among most native peoples the concept of "clan" exists. Loosely described
as "clan," a term which also is applied to Scots and other European
peoples, it refers to groups of people within a nation who are "born into" a
particular group, though not necessarily related by blood. Among the
Mohawk there are three clans—Turtle, Wolf and Bear. A person *always*
belongs to the clan of his or her mother. If a person from another nation
(including a white person) entered a tribal nation, that person had to be
adopted by a clan mother and was then of her clan. Among many native
nations, people were not supposed to marry someone of their own clan.
Further, if a member of the Bear Clan among the Mohawk, for example,
met a person of the Bear Clan from another native nation, she or he might

regard that person as a sister or a brother. Clans, therefore, created links between people and nations, as well as a sense of belonging to a special group.

Clan Animal. In most cases, a clan is said to have "come from" a particular animal. That animal is regarded as having a special relation to the members of that clan, who may even exhibit some of that animal's characteristics, such as being strong as the bear. These animals are regarded as ancestors and relatives, and many stories explain how a certain clan came to be when such an animal helped a human being long ago and then that person began that clan.

Clan Mother. Elder woman regarded as the head of a particular clan. Among matrilineal people such as the Haudenosaunee (Iroquois), a Clan Mother has great power and is a major political force. Among the Haudenosaunee, the women have a strong, central role. Each clan is headed by an elder woman, a Clan Mother, chosen by the others of her clan to lead. The Clan Mothers and the other women of the clan have many duties—such as choosing the men who will be "chiefs" among the Haudenosaunee. If a Haudenosaunee chief does not do his job well, the Clan Mother warns him three times and then, if he still fails to behave, she takes away his chieftaincy. The roles of Clan Mothers varied, and in some native nations of North America there were no Clan Mothers per se.

Comanche (Ko-man´-chē). Corruption of the Ute word *komon´teia*, "One Who Wants to Always Fight Me." A people of the southern Great Plains whose own name for themselves is *Nermurnuh* (New-mer´-noo) or "True Human Beings."

Coyote. Coyote is the trickster hero of many native stories throughout the west, southwest and northwest. Sometimes called "Old Man," he is regarded as both wise and foolish, dangerous and benevolent. Among some native people he is respected, while others regard him as untrustworthy. In this century, Coyote has become a sort of "Pan-Indian" symbol of native people themselves, and Coyote is the hero of many new contemporary tales that symbolize the struggle between native people and the government.

Cree (Krē). A primarily subarctic people whose various tribal nations stretch from Quebec in eastern Canada to Alberta in the west, a stretch of close to two thousand miles. In the area around Hudson Bay and James Bay, the traditional hunting and fishing subsistence lives of the Cree are threatened today by several James Bay power projects. The dams from these projects will block the major rivers of this region, creating a number of enormous lakes that will inundate much of that part of the North American continent, with disastrous ecological and cultural impacts.

Crow (Krō). Name usually applied to the native people of the northern Great Plains who call themselves *Absaroke* (Ahb-sah-rokuh), which means "Bird People," but could also mean "Crow."

da neho (dah ney-hō´) [Seneca] Literally "it is finished." A conventional way to end a story among the Iroquois.

Dakota (Dah-kō´-tah), [Sioux] One of the seven main "council fires" of the Sioux people. *Dakota* in the Santee Sioux dialect means "Allies" and refers to the Sioux of the eastern plains of Minnesota. Sioux called themselves *Ocheti Shakowin* (Oh-che-ti Shah-ko-win), "The Seven Council Fires."

Dine (Dih-nēy´), [Navajo] It means "The People."

Eskimo (Es´-kih-mō). Cree word meaning "Fish Eaters," applied to the people who call themselves *Inuit*—"The People."

Gitchee Manitou (Gih-chēe´ Man´-ē-too). [Anishinabe] The Great Spirit.

Grandmother. The term "grandmother" is used among many native people to refer in a respectful way to a female elder, whether human or animal.

Grandmother Spider. Grandmother Spider is a central character in many of the stories of the Southwest. She is seen in some stories as the Creator of many things. She introduced weaving to the people, and the rays of the sun are sometimes seen as part of her great web. She is a benevolent force in the native world of such people as the Dine (Navajo) and Pueblo nations.

Great League, "Iroquois." The alliance of peace forged among the formerly warring five nations of the Iroquois about five hundred or more years ago by The Peacemaker and Hiawatha. The Great League is still active among Iroquois peoples.

Great Spirit. A translation of various native names for the Creator, for example, the Anishinabe term *Gitchee Manitou* or the Abenaki term *Ktsi Nwaskw* (T-see´ Nah-wahsk´).

hageota (hah-gey´-oh-tah). [Iroquois] A person, usually a man in middle age, who travels from lodge to lodge telling stories and being rewarded for his efforts by being given small gifts, food and a place to stay.

Haida (Hī´-dah). Pacific northwest Indian group of Queen Charlotte Islands, British Columbia, and the southern end of Prince of Wales Island, Alaska. Called *Kaigani* in Alaska, they are known for their beautiful carvings, paintings and totem poles.

Haudenosaunee (Ho-dē-nō-show´-nē). [Iroquois] Iroquois name for themselves, which means "People of the Longhouse."

Hep owiy (Hep oh-wi-ēe´). [Hopi] Literally means "yes" or "uh-hunh."

Hero Twins. Hopi, Navajo and Pueblo traditional stories have these two playful and powerful children as heroes who kill monsters.

Hiii aya hiilyahahey (Hiii ah-yah´ hiii-yah´-ah-hey). [Hopi] Not translatable, a song made up of vocables like "tra-la-la" in English.

hogan (hō´-gun). [Navajo] Traditional dwelling made of logs and earth used by the Navajo.

Hopi (Hō´-pēe). Contraction of *Hopitu*, "The Peaceful Ones," the names used for themselves by a town-dwelling native people of north-eastern Arizona.

huih (hoo-ee´). [Hopi] An exclamation like "ah-hah."

huli-i-i, hu-li-i-i, pa shish lakwa-a-a-a (hoo-lee-e´-e hoo-lee-e´-e pah-sheesh´ lah-kwah´-ah-ah-ah . . .). [Zuni] Farewell song sung by the eagle.

Huya Ania (Hoo-yah´ Ah-nee´-ah). [Yaqui] "The wilderness world."

Iitoi (Ē´ -ē-toy). [Papago] Elder Brother, Our Creator.

inallaaduwi (in-ahl´-lah-ah´-doo-ee) [Achumawi] "People Not Connected to Anything." An Achumawi word for white people.

Inuit (In´-you-it), [Eskimo] "The People," name used for themselves by the native peoples of the farthest Arctic regions, Iceland and Arctic Asia. Not regarded by themselves or Indians as American Indian.

Inupiaq (I-noo´-pē-ak). One of the two major dialects of the Inuit (Eskimo) language spoken in Alaska. Inupiaq and Yupik are the two main Alaskan dialects of the Inuit language.

Iroquois (Ear´-oh-kwah). Corruption of an Algonquian word *ireohkwa*, meaning "real snakes." Applied commonly to the Six Nations, the "Haudenosaunee."

is ohi (ish o-hee´). [Hopi] Literally "oh my" or "oh dear."

kachina (kah-chee´-nah) [Hopi] Sacred dancers or spirit people who bring rain, equated with ancestors and clouds.

Kahionhes (Gah-hē-yōn´-heys). [Mohawk (Iroquois)] Name meaning "Long River."

Kiowa (Kī´-yō-wah). Native people of southern Great Plains (southwest Oklahoma). Name means "Principal People."

kiva (kē´-vah). [Hopi] A chamber, usually underground, used for ceremonies.

Kwakiutl (Kwah-kē´-yūt-ul). A people of the Pacific northwest, British Columbia coast. Sometimes referred to as *Kwaguilth* or *Kwa-Gulth*.

Lakota (Lah-kō´-tah) [Sioux] "Sioux" native people of northern plains, Nebraska, Dakotas. *See* Dakota.

Lakota Wiikijo Olowan (Lah-kō´-tah Wē-ē´-key-jō Oh-lo-wahn´). Lakota flute music.

lap lap (lap-lap) [Nez Percé] Butterfly.

Lapwai (Lap´-wī). [Nez Percé] "Valley of the Butterfly."

Little Loon or Mdawelasis (Meh-dah-wēē-lah-sis´). [Abenaki] The Abenaki name of Maurice Dennis, an Abenaki elder from the Adirondack region.

longhouse. Large traditional dwelling of Iroquois people. Framework of saplings covered with elm bark with central fires and, to each side, compartments for families.

madagenilhas (mah-dah´-gen-ill-has´). [Abenaki] Word for bat, literally "fur-hide bird."

Manabozho (Man-ah-bō´-zo). [Algonquian] Algonquian trickster hero, "Old Man."

medicine lodge. Small lodge used for curing ceremonies among northeastern native peoples.

Medicine Man. General term used to refer to "Indian doctors" who effect cures with a blend of psychiatry and sound herbal remedies, as well as by use of spiritual means. Each Indian nation has its own word for this person.

Megissogwon (Meh-gis-sog-wahn´). [Anishinabe] Anishinabe Spirit of Fever.

Miwok (Mee´-wohk). Native people of the part of California surrounding the San Francisco Bay area and east of the bay.

Mohawk (Mō´-hawk). Abenaki word *maquak*, used to refer to the Iroquois who lived in the area of Mohawk Valley in New York State and called themselves *Kanienkahageh* ("People of the Flint").

muktuk (muhk´-tuhk). The part of whale meat that includes the outer skin and the fat of the whale, also called "blubber."

Nanavits (Nah-navits´). [Paiute] "Moon of New Grass," month of April or May.

Native American. Native people of North, South and Central America who were aboriginal inhabitants prior to Columbus, and the descendants of these aboriginal inhabitants. Used interchangeably with the term "American Indian." In this book, we have used "Native North American" to refer to the native peoples of the United States and Canada.

Navajo (Nah´-vah-hō). *See* Dine.

Nez Percé (Nehz Purse). A native people of Idaho and western Washington. Name means "Pierced Nose" in French. The French confused the Nez Percé word for "themselves," *Choo-pin-it-pa-loo* ("People of the Mountain"), with the Nez Percé word *chopunnish* (pierced noses).

Nokomis (Nok-koh´-miss). [Anishinabe] "Grandmother," grandmother of Manabozho in stories.

Nootka (Nōōt´-kah). Maritime people of the coast of what is now called British Columbia.

nyaweh gowah (nēēy-ah´-way gō´-uh). [Kanienkahageh (Mohawk)] "Great thanks."

Oglala Sioux (Ō-glo´-lah Sōō). One of the branches of the western Lakota people.

Ojibway (Oh-jib´-wah). *See* Anishinabe.

Oneida (Oh-ny´-dah). [Iroquois] One of the Six Nations. Their name for themselves was *Onayatakono*, "People of the Standing Stone."

Onondaga (On-un-dah´-gah). [Iroquois] The centralmost of the six nations, the "Fire-keepers." Name for themselves is *Onundagaono*, "People on the Hills."

Osage (Ō´-sāj). The people who call themselves *Ni-U-kon´-Skah*, "The People of the Middle Waters." Their lands formerly included the area where Missouri, Kansas, Arkansas and Oklahoma meet, but today their communities are mostly in Osage County, Oklahoma.

Paiute (Pī´-yōōt). Native people of Nevada, Colorado, Arizona, California and Utah. The Northern Paiutes, sometimes referred to as the "Snakes," call themselves *Nu´ma* or *Ni´mi*, which means "People." The name *Paiute* is the modification of form borrowed into English and is probably misspelled.

Papago (Pah´-pah-gō). Southwest Indian group of southern Arizona. Nomadic horticulturalists and prolific basket weavers. Two-thirds of the roughly 13,500 Papagos today live on reservations located mostly in Pima County, Arizona, with some living in Sonora state, Mexico. Sometimes referred to as *Tohono O´odham*, "People of the Desert."

Pawnee (Paw-nēē´). A people of the northern Great Plains, Nebraska. Name may mean "Horn" or "Hunters." They call themselves *Chahiksichohiks*—"Men of Men."

Pit River Indian people. *See* Achumawi.

Pueblo (Pweb´-lō). [Spanish] Town, refers to a number of "town-dwelling" native peoples along the Rio Grande in New Mexico who live in large adobe buildings like apartment complexes.

qaade-wade toolol aakaadzi (kwah-ah-deh-wah-deh tool-ohl ah-ank-ah-dah-zee) [Achumawi] "The Beings Which Are World-over, All-living."

Raven. Raven is the trickster hero of many of the tales of the people of the Northwest. His image is usually carved on the top of totem poles of the region.

Santee Sioux (San´-tee Soo). A division of the eastern Dakota (Sioux) peoples living in Minnesota.

Sealth. *See* Chief Seattle.

Seneca (Sen´-eh-ka). Corruption of Algonquian word *O-sin-in-ka*, meaning "People of the Stone." Refers to the westernmost of the Six Nations, "Keepers of the Western Door." The Iroquois who called themselves *Nundawaono*, "People of the Great Hill."

Seye Wailo (Seh´-yeh Wa-e´-loh). [Yaqui] Literally "The Flower World," the mystically beautiful natural world inhabited by the deer in Yaqui stories and songs.

shaman (shah´-mun). An Asian term referring to one who speaks with ancestral spirits in order to heal or gain power. Often applied by Europeans to Native North American medicine men.

Shoshone (Sho-sho´-nee). Native people living in Wyoming, Nevada and parts of Utah. Also a term referring to the related nations of Shoshonean stock such as the Ute.

Sioux (Su). *See* Dakota. Corruption of an Anishinabe word meaning "Snakes," which refers to those who call themselves *Dakota* or *Lakota* or *Nakota* or *Ocheti Shakowin* (Oh-che-ti Shah-ko-win), "The Seven Council Fires."

Sitting Bull (1831–1890). Translation of the Hunkpapa Sioux name of *Tatanka Iyotake* (Tah-tan´-kah Ee-yo-tah´-kay), one of the great leaders of the Lakota people in the late 1800s.

Sonora. A state in northwest Mexico, also refers to the desert regions in southern Arizona.

Mount Tamalpais (Tam-ahl-pi´-us). California mountain, visible from the San Francisco area, which is a central feature in the Miwok creation story.

Tawa (Tah´-wah). [Hopi] The Sky God.

Tehanetorens (Dey´-ha-ne-do-lens) [Mohawk (Iroquois)] Name of Ray Fadden, an Iroquois Mohawk teacher; it means "He Is Looking Through the Pine Trees."

Teton Sioux (Te´-ton Soo). One of the western Lakota nations. Others included the Hunkpapa and the Oglala.

tipi (tee´pee). [Siouan] Plains Indian dwelling, a cone-shaped house of skins over a frame of poles; it means "dwelling."

Tirawa (Tee-rah´-wah). [Pawnee] The Creator.

Tlingit (Klin´-kit). A native people of the Pacific northwest.

totem (to´-tum). [Anishinabe] Refers to the animal relatives regarded as ancestral to the lineage. Each person is born into a particular totem, inherited in many native cultures through the mother. Totem animals include Bear, Eagle, Deer, Turtle, Wolf, Snipe, Eel and many others. Common throughout North America.

tribe. [From Latin *tribus*] A term used by both Indians and non-Indians to refer to groups of Native North Americans sharing a common linguistic and cultural heritage. Some Native North American people prefer to speak not of "tribe" but of *nation*.

Tsalagi. *See* Cherokee.

Tsimshian (Shim´-she̅-un). A native people of the Pacific northwest.

Turtle Clan. *See* Clan Animal, Bear Clan, clan.

Turtle Continent. North America, in many native stories, is placed on Great Turtle's back.

Tuscarora (Tus-ka-ro̅´-rah). The Sixth Nation of the Iroquois. The name means "Shirt-wearers." Driven by the Europeans from lands in North Carolina in the early eighteenth century, they resettled in western New York State.

Ute (Yo̅ot). Native people for whom the state of Utah is named. Their homeland included Colorado, Utah and part of New Mexico. An important division of the Shoshonean nations, most live today in Colorado. They call themselves *Nu Ci* (New´ Chi), which means "Person." The word *Ute* is a corruption of the Spanish term *Yuta*, which is of unknown origin.

Wabanaki Confederacy (Wa´-bah-na-ke̅e). A loose union of a number of Abenaki nations circa 1750–1850, possibly echoing an earlier confederacy and influenced by the Iroquois League. Allied Micmac, Maliseet, Passamaquoddy, Penobscot and Abenaki nations. Wampum belts were introduced and triannual meetings held at Caughnawaga, Quebec.

Wakan Tanka (Wah-kon´ Ton´-kah). [Lakota (Siouan)] The Creator. "The Great Mystery."

Wampanoag (Wom-pah-no̅´-ag). Means "Dawn People," sometimes called *Pokanoket*. Algonquian linguistic group of eastern woodlands, which once occupied what are now Bristol County, Rhode Island, and Bristol County, Massachusetts. Many were killed, along with the Narragansetts, by the colonists in King Philip's War in 1675 (King Philip was the colonists' name for Chief Metacomet, son of Massasoit). At least five hundred Wampanoag live today on Martha's Vineyard, Nantucket and other places in the region.

wampum (wom´-pum). Purple and white beads made from shells, they are still used by the Haudenosaunee as devices to record agreements between nations and to symbolize aspects of Iroquois history and culture. Woven together in strings in pre-Columbian times and then, after the introduction of European machinery, made into beads and strung into belts. *Not* used as money by native people.

water drum. Type of drum used by some northeastern native people such as the Iroquois. A small, round wooden drum shaped like a small pot, which has water placed in it to moisten the drum head and change the tone of the drum.

wica yaka pelo! (we̅e-chah´ yah´-kah pa̅´-low). [Dakota (Siouan)] "You have spoken truly" or "you are right."

wigwam (wig´-wom). [Abenaki] Probably from *wetuom*, which means "dwelling." Dome-shaped house made from bent sticks covered with bark, common to northeastern Abenaki peoples.

Yaqui (Yah´-kēē). Native people of Sonoran area of Mexico. Communities of Yaqui people also live in several regions of Arizona.

Yupik (Yōō´-pik). One of the Inuit (Eskimo) nations of the western coast of Alaska. Yupik and Inupiaq are the two main Alaskan dialects of the Inuit language. *Yupik* means "Authentic People." Yupik people are also found along the Siberian coast.

Zuni (Zōō´-ñēē). [ñ = nasalized] A Pueblo people of New Mexico who call themselves *Ashiwi*, "The Flesh." Name comes from a Keresan Pueblo word whose meaning is unknown.

Tribal Nation Descriptions

Anishinabe (Ah-nish-ih-nah'-bey)

The Anishinabe, or "The People," are also known as the Chippewa (in the United States) or the Ojibway (in Canada), names that may refer to the puckered style of moccasins they wore. A people of the central Great Lakes Region, they spoke an Algonquin language. Their houses were called wigwams. Most wigwams were single family dwellings, dome-shaped structures of bent and tied poles with bark covering. Large lodges, shaped something like an Iroquois longhouse, were also used for special ceremonial purposes such as the meetings of the members of the Midewiwin, a medicine society whose members had to devote their lives to serving the good of their people. (Mite wiwin means "medicine dance.") Elaborate pictographs drawn on birchbark were used by members of the Mide Society to remember songs and other texts.

Every Anishinabe person also belonged to a clan or "totem." Among the Anishinabe, clan was inherited from the father's side and, like the Iroquois, these clans were usually named after animals or birds. One was never supposed to marry someone from one's own clan.

Anishinabe material culture was based on the forest. Wood was used to make bows and arrows, bowls, snowshoes, flutes, drums, lacrosse sticks and many other things. Their baskets, the covering of their homes and the skins of their canoes were of birch bark, and much of their food was gathered from the forest, requiring them to live a seminomadic life. In the early spring, around March, they would set up camp near groves of maple trees to tap them for sugar, boiling the sap down in big wooden troughs. In the summer they would live in small villages where they gardened and gathered wild food and fished in an area with a radius of 40 miles or more. In the fall, they moved to the river and lakes and spent several weeks harvesting wild rice. To this day, Anishinabe people harvest wild rice. In the winter, they moved to their hunting grounds where the animal they most relied upon for food and for their clothing was the deer.

Their central culture hero is called Manabozho and there are hundreds of stories about him. In some stories he is heroic and in others he acts foolishly—

teaching proper behavior by showing what happens when you do the wrong thing. Manabozho is the actual hero of Longfellow's epic poem *Hiawatha*. Unfortunately, Longfellow mistakenly used the name of the Onondaga man who helped the Peacemaker found the League of the Iroquois. Making a historical Iroquois figure into a mythic Anishinabe hero is like telling the story of the Norse god Thor and calling him Charlemagne! (Sadly, mistakes such as Longfellow's can be found in many books about Native people.) Today the Anishinabe are among the most numerous of the Native people of North America, with about 160,000 living in communities in Michigan, Wisconsin, Minnesota, North Dakota and Southern Ontario. Some live on reservations, such as Turtle Mountain, White Earth and Leech Lake, but large communities of Anishinabe also exist in such cities as Minneapolis and St. Paul.

Apache (Ah-patch'-ē)

The name "Apache" comes from the Zuni word *apachu* which means "enemy." The various bands of the Apache people call themselves N'de or Tinde, which comes from their word *tinneh*, "The People." The Apache, until the late 1800s, led a somewhat nomadic existence. They used movable tipis or made small houses called *wickiups* from brush. These shelters could be erected quickly and easily as they moved on their seasonal migrations through their arid homelands which stretched in an 800-mile-long band south from Kansas into Mexico and 200 miles east from Oklahoma into Arizona. When certain bands migrated in the winter into the mountains, they would burn their wickiups leaving no trace of themselves behind. They grew corn and some other crops but relied more heavily on hunting and gathering. Raiding other tribal groups, such as the Pueblos (and later the Mexicans,) to get food and livestock was also viewed by the Apache as an important and legitimate way of sustaining themselves. As a result, they were often at odds with their neighbors.

Like their cousins, the Navajo, they speak an Athabascan tongue, closely related to languages spoken by Native peoples still living in the Arctic regions of Alaska and western Canada. It is generally accepted that the Apache migrated from the far north into the southwest sometime in the last thousand years. Their reputation as fierce fighters stems not only from their raiding the villages of the settled Pueblo peoples but also from their indomitable resistance to the U.S. government and the Spanish who sought to enslave them.

The Apache, especially the Chirichaua and the Mescalero bands, became widely known in the 1870s when they were confined by the U.S. government to reservations in Arizona and New Mexico and repeatedly tried to escape to their homelands in the mountains. Cochiose and Geronimo were among the most prominent of the leaders of the Apache resistance movement though at the time they were called "renegades." It is generally agreed today that the Apache resistance to American authority was due to unfairness and poor management on the part of the U.S. government when they removed these Native peoples from their traditional homelands to reservations where starvation and sickness were common. Today the four major Apache reservations of New Mexico and Arizona are among the more prosperous tribal communities in America. The White Mountain Apache of southeast Arizona, for example, have about 10,000 tribal members and run the thriving Sunrise Ski Resort. They also run a motel complex for visitors to White Mountain and share their culture each Labor Day weekend at the Apache Tribal Fair.

Cherokee (Chair-oh-kēy´)

The name the Cherokee use for themselves is Ani-un-wiya, which means "The Principal People." They also call themselves Tsa-la-gi (which became "Cherokee"), derived from the Choctaw *chiluk-ki*, which means "Cave Dwellers." The Cherokee, along with the Choctaw, the Chickasaw, the Creek and the Seminole (who were, themselves, a branch of the lower Creek Nation) were called the "Five Civilized Tribes" because they sucessfully adopted white ways. The fact that they were only called "civilized" because they had taken on certain culture traits from the European-based immigrants is an expression of the enthnocentric attitudes toward Native people held by the white culture.

Their homeland was the central Appalachian mountains. They lived in large villages along the banks of the rivers. Each village had a large council house and a central plaza for political meetings and ceremonies. Their individual homes and the council house were usually made of wattle, woven saplings covered with mud. The conical Cherokee house was called the *asi*. In the summer, the Cherokee people would move out of their wattle houses to live in open-sided shelters. The typical head-covering for a Cherokee man was not a feathered cap, but a wrapped turban, sometimes decorated with one or more tall feathers.

Like their northern cousins, the Iroquois, the Cherokee people were matrilineal and matrilocal. They also relied upon deer and corn as their main sources of food. They closely observed the animals of the forest and in many of their stories, like the tale of the possum, those animals gather together in council just as the Cherokee do.

Of the southern Native nations, the Cherokee was the largest. In the 1700s, their lands covered 70 million acres across what is now Tennessee, Georgia, Alabama and North Carolina. By the late 1700s, they had given up their old style of house and adopted to white ways. A man named Sequoia codified the Cherokee language (using, some say, a script in use since pre-Columbian times by Cherokee medicine people) and by 1820, more than half of the 17,000 Cherokees could read and write their own language. Aside from using their own language and keeping certain of their customs, the Cherokee were hard to distinguish from their white neighbors. They had newspapers, banks, schools, farms, wore white clothing and got along well with most of their non-Indian neighbors.

What happened next is one of the saddest and most shameful stories in American history. Gold was discovered on Cherokee land in 1827. The state of Georgia then claimed the Indian lands as part of its state wealth. The Cherokees were ordered to leave and the other states of the south did the same to the other four civilized tribes. Led by Chief John Ross, the Cherokees fought the case in the courts. In the end, the U.S. Supreme Court decided that removal of the Cherokees was not legal. They had a right to remain on their own land. Shamefully, President Andrew Jackson supported the Indian Removal Act of 1830. "The Supreme Court has made their decision," President Jackson said, "now let them enforce it."

Some Cherokees went voluntarily to the land designated as Indian Territory (the current state of Oklahoma). More than 15,000 refused to leave. Finally, in 1838, soldiers were sent to forcibly remove the Cherokees from their homes, their farms and their lands. More than four thousand Cherokees died along the way to Oklahoma on what came to be called The Trail of Tears. Among those who died was Quatie Ross, wife of the principal Cherokee chief, who gave her blanket to a freezing child.

A number of Cherokee people escaped into the hills of North Carolina. As a result, the Cherokee nation of today is divided between the Cherokees of Oklahoma and the smaller Eastern Band of Cherokees in North Carolina, which numbers about six thousand. Other Cherokee people and their descendents are scattered all over the continent. The majority of Cherokees, more than fifty thousand by the last census, live in Oklahoma, which became the U.S. dumping ground for many other dispossessed tribal nations throughout the 1800s. (In the last act of betrayal, even "Indian territory" was taken from the Indians in the early 1900s and made into the state of Oklahoma.) The Cherokee Nation of Oklahoma, which is currently headed by Chief Wilma Mankiller, has its capital in Tahlequah. The tribal offices there can provide information to visitors about their heritage center and festivals open to the public. The Eastern Cherokee offer much to vistors who come to Cherokee, North Carolina, including a museum, a reconstructed village, craftspeople demonstrating and selling their traditional works and an annual pageant offered all summer called "Unto These Hills," portraying the history of the Cherokee.

Choctaw (Chock'-taw)

The Choctaw people were one of the largest of the tribal nations of the Southeast. Their traditional homeland is in that area of lowlands, deltas, swamps and rivers now known as Mississippi. The name "Choctaw" is thought by some to derive from the Spanish word *chato*, "flat," a reference to the Choctaw practices of flattening their heads. Traditionally, the Choctaw relied upon council meetings to make their decisions. Their system of government was a highly democratic one, with three districts and three principal chiefs, called *Mingos*, elected by the men of each district. At national council meetings, those chiefs, the war chiefs (who were subordinate to them) and the other elected officials gathered around to discusss the business of the Choctaw nation. Of all of the southern tribes, the Choctaws were regarded as the best farmers. Early European visitors to the Choctaws remarked upon the great expanses of farm land. They had an intimate knowledge of the animals and wild plants of the swamps and bayous—as the two stories in *Keepers of the Animals* indicate—but they spent less time hunting than did their neighbors farther north. Because they did not need to migrate seasonally to find food, relying on the harvest of corn and other crops and because the land was so fertile, Choctaw houses tended to be permanent, made of logs and stucco, and grouped closely together. Although the majority of the Choctaw people were removed to Oklahoma, some avoided resettlement, and there is still a thriving Choctaw Nation existing on a 21,000-acre reservation in east central Mississippi. Today there are about twenty thousand Choctaw in Oklahoma and five thousand in Mississippi.

Oklahoma, which means "People of Red Earth," is itself a Choctaw word. In Oklahoma each Labor Day, the Choctaw people hold an open festival in Tuskahoma, including a traditional stickball game. In Philadelphia, Mississippi, the Mississippi Band of the Choctaw Nation puts on a four-day Choctaw Indian Fair beginning the first Wednesday after July 4 and featuring the Choctaw Stickball World Series.

Cree (Krē)

The Cree are the most widespread of the Native nations of the subarctic, found in a wide band that stretches below and around Hudson Bay, almost from one side of the continent to the other. Where wide expanses of treeless swampy muskeg and frozen tundra are edged by the boreal coniferous forest. It is an area where great herds of migratory caribou have been the mainstay of many Native peoples. The other mammals that have been a source of life to the Cree include the moose and the varying hare. The Cree people also trap, fish the streams and, along the seashores, make use of the ocean environment. Agriculture is not possible because of the brief growing season. There is widespread understanding among the Cree that their lives depend upon the animals for their survival.

One of the most respected of the animals is the bear. When a bear is killed its skull is usually reverentially placed in a tree in the belief that the animal's spirit will be pleased and will not prevent success in future hunting. As the Cree story of hunting the moose shows, it is only through the proper relationship between hunter and animal that the balance can be kept.

Low dome- or tipi-shaped wigwams, sod houses and wooden shelters are among the traditional homes made by the Cree people. Birch bark is widely used for basketry and for the covering of houses and canoes. Warm-layered clothing is made from animal skins. Their use of snowshoes, snow goggles and toboggans is well-adapted for the subarctic regions.

Unfortunately, the Cree and other Native peoples of Eastern Canada are threatened with the destruction of their environment and their cultures by a number of gigantic hydroelectric projects. The East Main Cree and the West Main Cree, located on either side of Hudson's Bay, number more than ten thousand people who have already been drastically affected. The dams constructed thus far in Phase One of the James Bay Project—which is selling its electricity to the

United States—have flooded expanses of land bigger than some of the New England states. The water is now dangerously polluted by natural mercury that the flood waters have released from the soil, poisoning an entire ecosystem and filling the fish that the Cree people feed upon with so much mercury contamination that eating too many fish may now cause death. The Audubon Society and many other responsible organizations agree with the Cree and Inuit peoples who are fighting to stop its progress that this man-made change of the lands and waters of the north may be the greatest ecological disaster of the twentieth century.

Dakota (Dah-kō'-tah)

See *Sioux*.

Haida (Hī'-dah)

The homelands of the Haida people are the Queen Charlotte Islands of present-day British Columbia on the northwestern Pacific Coast of Canada. Famed for their boat-building and wood-carving, these peoples of the Pacific Northeast have the same sort of relationship with the salmon that the Plains nations do with the American bison. The Haida have depended on the ocean for centuries to supply most of their food. They have been as familiar with the waters of their rivers, their many bays and the open ocean as other Native people with the land. Their stories of the salmon show how close a relationship they felt to their nonhuman relatives.

Traditionally, the Haida are equally dependent upon the great forests of their coastal region, using the cedars, in particular, for their large houses, their canoes, boxes, masks, totem poles and many other items. Some of their canoes are large enough to hold forty or more people. The beauty and originality of the carvings of the Haida are world-reknowned.

Whenever a tree was cut, its spirit was thanked for its sacrifice and in some cases, planks would be cut from the living tree without killing it. The totem poles depict characters out of Haida stories and the histories of their various nations. Raven, who is a trickster figure capable of great heroism and great foolishness, is often carved at the top of the totem poles, while such other beings as the killer whale, frog, beaver and bear are also frequently portrayed.

Haudenosaunee (Ho-dē-nō-show'-nē)

The Haudenosaunee or Iroquois. An early confederation of five Native Nations, the Iroquois had highly developed diplomacy and what might be called an "international culture." Iroquois traditions speak of migration from the west to their present homes in the areas now known as New York State, and the Canadian provinces of Ontario and Quebec.

The three Iroquois stories in *Keepers of the Animals* come from two of the five original nations of the Iroquois league. Those five nations were the Mohawk, the Oneida, the Onondaga, the Cayuga and the Seneca. (When their lands were taken from them by white settlers, the Tuscarora people migrated north from North Carolina and were allowed to join the Iroquois League as the 6th Nation.) Their confederacy was known as the Great League, and it was symbolized by a giant white pine tree, the Tree of Peace. On the top of the tree, an eagle holding five bundled arrows—a symbol of strength in unity—in its claws watched for any threat to the peace. (That same symbol is found on the U.S. quarter—borrowed from the Iroquois, whose league is now credited by many historians as having a direct influence on the formation of American democracy and the Constitution.)

The Iroquois relied on both agriculture and hunting to feed their people. Their stories and ceremonies of Thanksgiving honor both the animals and the plants. Instead of one Thanksgiving, the Iroquois have Thanksgiving several times throughout the year, each ceremony at a time when some event in the natural world—such as the ripening of the corn or the gathering of maple syrup—deserves thanks.

The dwellings of the Iroquois people were called longhouses. (Haudenosaunee means "People of the Longhouse.") The longhouses were often huge, their roofs taller than two men, buildings big enough to hold as many as twenty or more families in apartments on either side of the central fires. Long inner walls running north to south created a corridor in the middle. The arched roof was vented with smokeholes for the central fires, which provided heat in the cold seasons and were used by everyone for cooking. Typically, a longhouse was inhabited by the people of a single clan and headed by an elder Clan Mother. There were many clans among the Iroquois named after the birds and animals who were regarded as friends and relations of the people. The three clans found among all of the five Iroquois Nations were Turtle, Bear and Wolf.

Among the Iroquois—and most other Native nations in North America—women were very powerful and equal to the men in terms of influence and respect. Iroquois women were responsible for agriculture and were the owners of the longhouses. Clan was inherited from the mother's side (making them matrilineal), and when a man married he went to live with his wife's clan. (This made them a matrilocal people—residency controlled and decided by the mother's side.) The women also decided which of the men of their clan would represent them as Faithkeepers (the equivalent, one might say, of senators or representatives) at the meetings of the Great League. If a man did not behave properly when he was a representative, the women of his clan would warn him three times. After the third warning, the woman would symbolically "remove his horns," taking him from office. Because the Great League was a League of Peace, formed long ago by a man known as The Peacemaker at a time when the Iroquois nations were fighting each other, no Representative to the League was allowed to fight in war, and anyone who had been a warrior could never be a Faithkeeper.

Hopi (Hō'-pēē)

Their name is a contraction of Hopitu, "The Peaceful Ones." The Hopi are, indeed, a people of peace. They have a long history of resolving conflicts through means other than warfare. Their extremely sophisticated knowledge of dryland farming has enabled them to survive in the arid mesa regions of what is now northern Arizona, where many of their multilevel, multiple-residency buildings of adobe and wood have been continuously inhabited for more than five hundred years. The artistic traditions of the Hopi include weaving and pottery, both of which were given to them by the benevolent Grandmother Spider, who is seen as one of the primary creative forces. Hopi traditional stories and prophecies speak of past worlds destroyed as a result of misdeeds and warn of future cataclysm if human beings do not follow a way of life in balance with the natural world and all of its beings. The ten thousand members of the Hopi Nation today live primarily on three mesas in the midst of a one-and-a-half-million-acre piece of land which is completely surrounded by the huge Navajo Reservation.

Inupiaq (In-nōō'-pē-yak)

Inuit, (who call themselves Inupiaq or Inupiat in Alaska) live in the far north. Many families have relatives on both the Asian and the American sides of the Siberian land bridge. The Inuit people are found widely across the far north, including Siberia, Alaska, Canada and Greenland.

Although the Arctic climate is harsh—a land of no trees and, where there is earth, the ever-present permafrost is only a few inches below the surface even at the height of summer—the Inuit live full lives in balance with their environment. These Native people of the far north distinguish themselves from the "American Indian," regarding themselves as being of another race. Inuit or Inupiaq is a word meaning "Real People." They also have been popularly called "Eskimo," a name first applied to the eastern Canadian Inuit by the French in 1584 and spelled by them "Esquimaux." Eskimo is a word that apparently comes from an Eastern Algonquin language and the exact meaning of it is not clear, though it may refer to the making of snowshoes. The word does not mean "raw meat eaters," though the *Oxford English Dictionary* tells us this.

The Inuit people are found in a band of habitation that stretches across northern Asia and Northern America, including Greenland, where they were called not Eskimos but "Greenlanders" for many centuries before Columbus came to America. There are many different Inuit groups around the Arctic, who speak in varying dialects. However, they recognize their kinship and in 1977 at the Inuit Circumpolar Conference in Alaska adopted the name "Inuit" to apply to all peoples once called "Eskimo."

A knowledge of the animals of ocean and land is vital for survival in the far north, as is an attitude of respect and gratitude. When an Inuit hunter spears a seal, he will fill his mouth with fresh water and then give that water to the dead animal, in the belief that it has allowed itself to be killed in exchange for that drink.

The efficient clothing of the Inuit; their methods for hunting caribou, seal, walrus and whale; their shelters built of driftwood, whalebones, snow and ice; their dog sleds; even a type of "sunglasses" worn to screen their eyes from the glare of the ice and avoid snowblindness have all been developed over thousands of years as a result of surviving by living close to nature. Though there are cultural differences over the broad expanse of their regions, there are many distinctively Inuit practices. These include methods of winter travel over tundra and sea ice, hunting and fishing techniques for capturing marine and land animals, specialized tool designs, unique social customs and strong oral traditions. They are well-known for their use of skin boats, harpoons, oil lamps and spear throwers. Their beautiful carvings of stone and walrus ivory and bone are now seen in galleries all over the world, and it has been widely acknowledged that their shamans show a deep knowledge of human psychology and of effective medical practice.

The major comings of European culture to the Inuit probably began with a colony founded by the Norse in Greenland in the year 982. Subsequent changes, especially in the twentieth century, have brought certain conveniences to the Inuit peoples such as outboard motors, rifles, snowmobiles and radios, but have also brought social and economic influences that have disrupted the pattern of their cultures. The development of oil resources in Alaska has also brought many formerly isolated communities into regular contact with Western civilization. However, the contemporary Inuit people are attempting to survive by combining the new with the old and by making their reliance upon nature and their respect for it and central part of their new way of life. Hunting the bowhead whale still goes in several coastal communities of northern Alaska, and it is regulated by the Inupiaq Whaling Corporation so that no more than a few whales are killed each year. Inuit groups from all over the Arctic meet regularly at Inuit Circumpolar Conferences which are held in different locations each year. These meeting consider such things as the continuance of the Inuit way of life and the threats to the fragile environment of the far North being posed by Western development and pollution. There is also an "Eskimo Olympics" held each year in Alaska that attracts contestants in such events of strength and agility as leaping from a standing position to pick a ball hung 10 feet overhead or carrying six men on your back for a set distance—each of which mimics those skills needed for hunting and survival.

Iroquois (Ear'-oh-kwah)

See *Haudenosaunee*.

Kiowa (Kī'-yō-wah)

The Kiowa people migrated onto the plains within the last five hundred years from their original homes near the upper Yellowstone and Missouri rivers. They allied themselves with the Crow people and continued south, eventually settling in the area we now know as western Oklahoma and allying themelves with the Comanche people. The Comanche, Cheyenne and Kiowa carried on warfare with the frontier settlements of Mexico and Texas, trying in vain to stop both further settlement and the destruction of the buffalo. The "Buffalo War" continued until the late 1800s when the buffalo were destroyed, and the Native people were forced onto reservations.

Today, though their reservation lands were taken from them when the state of Oklahoma was formed, the Kiowa people still reside in southwestern Oklahoma. Their current tribal rolls number more than five thousand people. One of the most famous of contemporary Kiowas is N. Scott Momaday, a writer who relies strongly on the old storytelling traditions, and whose novel *House Made of Dawn* won the Pulitzer Prize. His book *The Way to Rainy Mountain* tells of the migration and survival of the Kiowas. The Kiowa have also become well known in recent years for their artistic ability and there are a number of famous Kiowa painters. The Kiowa Tribal Museum is located in Carnegie, Oklahoma.

Lakota (Lah-kō'-tah)
See *Sioux*.

Miwok (Mee'-wohk)
Their name, Miwok, simply means "Human." Their traditional lands stretched along the California coast from the area near San Francisco north through what is now Sacramento. They fished, hunted, gathered and stored acorns and seeds to see them through the mild winter months. Highly developed arts of basketry and their extremely complex stories about the Creation and the relationships of the animal people to each other and to human beings are among the evidences of the high artistic and intellectual abilities of these first native Californians. Material possessions, including clothing, tended to be very few. Their houses, which held six to 10 people, were cone-shaped, a frame of saplings or driftwood covered with grass bunches bound together and tied on like shingles. Further inland, the Miwok people made houses with bark shingles and constructed large roundhouses supported by four center posts and covered with branches and dirt so that they resembled small hills. These roundhouses, which were as much as 50 feet in diameter, were used for social and ritual gatherings. Among the Miwok people the roles of men and women in running their villages seem to have been quite equal. Tattooing was practiced by women and men, with the most common tattoos being straight lines drawn from the chin to the stomach. Dancing—as it is today among many other California Native peoples— was common and frequent, both for fun and for special ceremonial occasions. Like many other of the Native nations of the West Coast, the favorite character in their stories is Coyote, the Trickster.

The Russians and the Spanish both came to the California coast and engaged in conflict with the original inhabitants, but it was the Spanish who did the most destruction. The Spanish mission system led to a forced labor system which cause widespread changes and the deaths of many Native people. Many parts of the West Coast were virtually depopulated by the Spanish, and when the area became an American possession and the gold rush of the mid-1800s occurred, many of the smaller tribal nations of the West Coast were wiped out. However, California Native culture was not wiped out. Today, California ranks third among all of the states in the U.S. in Native population. There are three Miwok tribal councils and at the Kule Loklo Miwok Indian Village near Olema dance celebraions open to the public are held each summer. The Tuolumne Indian Rancheria offers an annual Mi-Wuk Indian Acorn Festival in September.

Mohawk (Mō'-hawk)

See *Haudenosaunee.*

Nootka (Nōōt'-kah)

The Nootka are a group of related peoples of the Pacific northwest along the coast of what is now British Columbia. Boat-builders, woodcarvers, fishermen and hunters of the whale, their traditional way of life was much like that of the Haida, emphasizing an understanding of the ocean as a source of their lives.

The Nootka practiced giveaway ceremonies that were even more complex than those found in many other parts of the continent. (Among a great many of the Native peoples of North America, giving away your personal possessions is a way to show your thanks for good fortune.) The Potlatch ceremony was a giveaway of grand proportions. The word potlatch comes from the Nootka word *patshatl*, which means "giving." The potlatch has been described by anthropologists as a "competition," but this was not the case among the Nootka who avoided the competitive element and stressed mutuality. The potlatch served as an exchange to strengthen the solidarity of the people. The customs of giveaways and potlatches served a useful social function in that they prevented the accumulation of too much wealth in the hands of any one person and promoted sharing among the people. Because the concept of such free giving and sharing of valuable goods was counter to the European ideas of individual property owning and investment, the potlatch was made illegal by the Canadian government from the early 1900s to 1951.

Osage (Ōh'-sāj)

"Osage" is a corruption of Wazhazhe, an Osage word meaning "True People." Their homelands are the eastern edge of the American plains in the tallgrass prairies of the area now known as eastern Kansas and western Missouri. Until the horse came, they did some hunting of the buffalo, but relied more heavily on agriculture, making use of the fertile lands along the rivers to grow their corn.

The Osage, even though they generally stood well over 6 feet (early French visitors to the Osage people met some Osage men who were 7 feet tall!) called themselves "The Little Ones" to show their humility to Honga, "The Sacred One," Mother Earth. They regarded the animals around them as relatives and teachers, and they passed down their traditions, which often were about the animals and the other wise beings of the natural world in long prose poems which they called the *wi-gi-es*. The story of how the spider symbol came to them is found in one of those long epic traditions.

Relatives of the Omaha, Ponca and Quapaw, the Osage people were resettled by the U.S. government in Indian Territory. There are over six thousand registered members of the Osage tribe today and their tribal offices are located in Pawhuska, Oklahoma.

Papago (Pah'-pah-gō)

The name Papago means, literally, "The Bean People," and is a reflection of the way these people, wise in the ways of the desert, have relied upon the beans of such plants as mesquite for their food. Along with their cousins, the Pima, they call themselves *O'odham*, which means "The People." In addition to gathering a surprisingly wide variety of foods from the desert plants, they also made use of irrigation to grow cotton, corn and beans. Their dome-shaped lodges, perhaps 15 feet in diameter and made of a frame of saplings and thatched with leaves, blended seamlessly into the landscape.

More than seventeen thousand Papago people remain in their homeland in the Sonoran desert near what is now Tucson, Arizona, and there is also a sizable population in Sonora, Mexico. They are well-known today among art collectors for their complex and beautiful basketry and agronomists have recently begun to listen carefully to what the Papago still have to tell them about the best ways to sustain agriculture in the desert.

Seneca (Sen'-eh-ka)

See *Haudenosaunee*.

Sioux (Su)

Perhaps the best-known Native peoples of North America today are the people popularly known as the Sioux. (Sioux is a name that comes from the Anishinabe word *Nadowe-is-iw*, a word that means "snakes," indicating the Sioux were their enemies.) They called themselves either Dakota or Lakota, depending on whether they spoke the Eastern or the Western dialect of their languages and also referred to themselves as *Ocheti Lakowin*, "The Seven Council Fires."

In the popular imagination, the Sioux look the way Indians "should look." Their tipis, feathered headdresses, chivalric warriors, buffalo hunting and horse culture became, with the help of movies and television, the image of the Native

American in the public eye. There is no doubt that their traditional way of life, which stressed—for both men and women—the virtues of generosity, honor, personal courage, fortitude, cooperation and the careful use of the natural world's gifts, is very admirable. Those qualities are reflected in their stories. Sadly, the continuing history of the relations of the U.S. government with the Sioux nations reflects how little the United States has understood or respected these proud and highly principled people.

Formerly living along the Mississippi River, the Sioux spread into the plains with the advent of the horse. By the 1800s their territory stretched from what is now Minnesota through the present-day states of North Dakota, South Dakota, Nebraska and Montana. Their fierce defense of their homes against the encroachment of white civilization and the eloquence of such leaders as Sitting Bull and Red Cloud (both of whom inflicted major defeats upon the U.S. Army) brought them squarely into the public eye from the mid-1800s on. The massacre of unarmed Sioux people by U.S. Army troops at Wounded Knee in 1890 is an event that marked the end of the military campaigns against the Native peoples of North America and forced the remaining Native nations of the Plains onto reservations. Those campaigns against the Native people also coincided with a concerted and successful effort by the U.S. government to wipe out the great herds of American bison, thus cutting off the food supply of such Native peoples as the Kiowa and Sioux who were successful at resisting white domination as long as they had the buffalo to rely upon.

Despite these hardships, the nations of the plains have survived and, in the 1990s, gathered strength. There are more than forty thousand Sioux people today and the Sioux and other Native nations have engaged in litigation to return to them some of the land taken illegally in the late 1800s and early 1900s—in particular the sacred Black Hills of South Dakota. There are small buffalo herds reestablished in a number of places throughout the plains, and one radical proposal by contemporary non-Native ecologists is that much of the northern plains area should be returned to its original state as a gigantic national park where the buffalo and other native species of plants and animals can return.

Tlingit (Klin'-kit)

Their name means "The People." The Tlingit people are located in the area now known as southeastern Alaska and the southwest Yukon and northwest British Columbia. Their staple food was and remains fish and, like the other northwest peoples, they are reknowned as woodworkers. Their communal houses made of cedar logs were often large enough to hold several hundred people. Famous as warriors and traders, they defended their coastal lands fiercely, repelling the Russians when they tried to invade centuries ago. They boast a highly developed oratorical tradition which has been the subject of several books coauthored by Nora Dauenhauer, a contemporary Tlingit writer.

A matriarchal society, the Tlingit have two main divisions, Ravens and Wolves, with smaller clan groups inside each division. They believed, along with their neighbors, that these divisions were related to each other, exclusive of tribe. This meant, for example, that Tlingits of the Eagle Division regarded themselves as relatives of Haidas of the Eagle Division and could go and visit those Haida Eagles and be welcomed as relatives—even though their languages were different and they were strangers. In addition to their carving of totem poles, boxes and masks, the Tlingit are known for their famous Chilkat blankets made of cedar bark and mountain goat hair. There are about ten thousand Tlingits living in Alaska today.

Yaqui (Yah'-kēē)

The Yaqui people are more recent arrivals to the United States area of the southwest. The bulk of the Yaqui people once lived in small settlements along the Yaqui river in what is now called Sonora in Mexico. They lived as farmers and made great use of the resources of the desert around them. The Yaqui people are deeply connected to the desert and regard it as a beautiful, magical place, a place of flowers, a place of the deer people. Their resistance in the late 1800s to the lawlessness of the Mexican people who invaded their lands resulted in the occupation of their part of Sonora by the Mexican army and the diaspora of the Yaqui people. They were even more dispersed than were the Cherokee. Many came to the United States as refugees. A community of several thousand Yaquis can be found in Arizona, primarily in four settlements in Phoenix and Tucson. In Tucson, the Yaqui Deer Dances are an attraction for tourists who admire their spectacular costumes and music, even if they know little of Yaqui history or traditions. Performed at festivals throughout the year, one of the best times to see the Yaqui Deer Dance is Holy Week before Easter Sunday.

Zuni (Zōō'-ñēē)

The Zuni call themselves Siwi, "People." Their traditional lands are along the banks of the Zuni River, in the 200-square-mile area west of the Continental Divide on the border between New Mexico and Arizona. The Zuni have dwelled for thousands of years in settled communities near or not far from the Rio Grande in large adobe-brick complexes of apartments arranged around a central plaza.

The Zuni are urban, settled agriculturists. The complexity of their ritual life and mythology is unparalleled on this continent and, to this day, their ceremonies and those of the other Pueblo nations that remain open to the public are striking in their beauty and power. Their overall purpose is to maintain the harmony of the world. Many of their ceremonies are closed to outsiders, but the great early winter celebration of Shalako, one of the most spectacular of all Native ceremonies remains open to all who come.

They are among the world's greatest dryland farmers, growing varieties of corn, beans and squash which have been developed over the centuries to thrive in near-desert conditions using techniques that vary from deliberate irrigation to the wise use of scarce naturally occurring water supplies and runoff.

They were the first of the Pueblo peoples to be visited by the Spanish when Coronado attacked them in 1540. The Spanish believed that one of the Zuni towns, Hawikuh, was one of the fabled "Seven Cities of Gold of Cibola," filled with gold and silver like the cities of the Aztecs and Incas. Such cities never existed, but the Spanish persisted in calling the area "Cibola" for many years. The invasion of the Spanish and their harsh domination of the Pueblo peoples from about 1598 on—wiping out whole villages, condemning traditional practices as witchcraft and making slaves of many of the people—resulted in the great Pueblo Revolt of August 10, 1680. Careful plans were made by Pope, a man of San Juan Pueblo, and runners were sent from Pueblo to Pueblo. All of the people rose up on the same day and the Spanish were driven out of the region for more than a decade. Though the Spanish reconquered the area, the Spanish had learned a lesson from their own mistakes and were more moderate in their rule. The present-day population of Zuni is about seven thousand people, making them the largest of all the Pueblo nations.

Other Versions of Native North American Stories

In choosing the stories to be included in *Keepers of the Animals* and in its predecessor *Keepers of the Earth*, I followed several rules. The first was to choose stories with levels of meaning relatively easy for a general audience to understand. (Each of these stories also may have additional levels of meaning that can only be perceived by those who are extremely close to the individual tribal nation each story comes from.) The second rule was to not tell "restricted" stories, stories only to be shared with those who are, in some way, "initiated." My third rule was to include only stories with earlier versions already in print or in public circulation through recordings or film. I do not wish to be the first to take a story out of the oral tradition. By this I do not mean to condemn those who first "document" such stories; I simply mean to make it clear that I do not see this as my role. Fourth, the versions included in this book (and in *Keepers of the Earth*) are my own retellings and may differ considerably from other versions already recorded. In general, this is because I have tried to make my versions closer to the oral traditions from which the stories come or to include important information left out in other recorded tellings.

The following list will lead the reader to some (but not all) other versions of many of the stories in *Keepers of the Animals*.

Silver Fox and Coyote Create Earth (Miwok). Those who have drawn on California Indian stories of Fox and Coyote include Mohawk poet Peter Blue Cloud. See Peter Blue Cloud, *Elderberry Flute Song* (Fredonia, N.Y.: White Pine Press, 1989). Other versions are Jane Louis Curry, *Back in the Beforetime* (New York: Macmillan, 1987); Jamie de Angulo, *Coyote Man and Old Doctor Loon* (San Francisco, Calif.: Turtle Island Foundation, 1973); and a compilation by Edward Gifford and Gwendoline Harris Block, *California Indian Nights* (Lincoln: University of Nebraska Press, 1990).

How the People Hunted the Moose (Cree). One of the best collectors of Cree traditions has been Howard Norman, whose books range from *The Wishing Bone Cycle* (New York: Stonehill Press, 1976) to a 1990 collection of traditional stories from the north. This particular story is found among the Abenaki and other

Algonquin-speaking people. Versions include *Legends from the Forest*, told by Chief Thomas Fiddler (Moonbeam, Ontario: Penumbra Press, 1985).

How Grandmother Spider Named the Clans (Hopi). Other versions are found in G.W. Mullett, *Spider Woman Stories* (Tucson: University of Arizona, 1979); Edmund Nequatewa, *Truth of a Hopi* (Flagstaff, Ariz.: Northland Press, 1967); Frank Waters, *The Book of the Hopi* (New York: Viking Press, 1963); and *Meditations With the Hopi* (Santa Fe, N.M.: Bear & Company, 1986).

How the Spider Symbol Came to the People (Osage). Other versions are found in Robert Liebert, *Osage Life and Legends* (Happy Camp, Calif.: Naturegraph, 1987); and Francis LaFlesche, *The Osage Tribe* (Washington, D.C.: Bureau of American Ethnology Report 35, 1918).

The Rabbit Dance (Mohawk). Other versions are found in J.N.B. Hewitt, *Onondaga Mohawk and Seneca Myths* (Washington, D.C.: Bureau of American Ethnology Report 21, 1910–11); and Tehanetorens, *Tales of the Iroquois* (Mohawk Nation via Rooseveltown, N.Y.: Akwesasne Notes, 1976).

The Deer Dance (Yaqui). Other versions are found in Refugio Savala, *Autobiography of a Yaqui Poet* (Tucson: University of Arizona Press, 1980); and Larry Evers and Felipe S. Molina, *Yaqui Deer Songs/Maso Bwikam* (Tucson: University of Arizona Press, 1987).

Eagle Boy (Zuni). This story is found among more than one of the Pueblo nations. A Hopi version can be found in G.M. Mullett, *Spider Woman Stories.* Other Zuni versions are Frank Hamilton Cushing, *Zuni Folk Tales* (Tucson: University of Arizona Press, 1901); and the Zuni people, *The Zunis: Self-Portrayals* (Albuquerque: University of New Mexico, 1972).

Turtle Races with Beaver (Seneca). Versions of this tale are found among all of the Six Nations of the Iroquois and in various neighboring tribal nations such as the Lenape and the Abenaki. Two sources are Arthur C. Parker, *Skunny Wundy, Seneca Indian Tales* (Chicago: Albert Whitman and Co., 1970) and William M. Beauchamp, *Iroquois Folk Lore* (Port Washington, N.Y.: Kennikat Press, 1966).

Octopus and Raven (Nootka). Other versions are found in Franz Boaz, "The Nootka" (6th Report on the Indian Tribes of Canada, 1890); and David W. Ellis and Luke Swan, *Teachings of the Tides* (Nanaimo, B.C.: Theytus Books, 1981).

How the Butterflies Came to Be (Papago). Other versions are found in *American Indian Myths and Legends*, selected and edited by Richard Erdoes and Alfonso Ortiz (New York: Pantheon, 1984); and Mary I. Neff, "Pima and Papago Legends," (*Journal of American Folklore* 25, 1912).

Salmon Boy (Haida). This story is widely told among the various tribal nations of the northwest coast including the Kwakiutl, the Tlingit and the Klallum. Versions include John Bierhorst, *The Mythology of North America* (New York: Quill, 1985); and John R. Swanton, *Contributions to the Ethnology of the Haida* (New York: American Museum of Natural History, 1905).

The Woman Who Married a Frog (Tlingit). Another version is by John R. Swanton, *Tlingit Mythos and Tales* (Washington, D.C.: Bureau of American Ethnology Report 39, 1909).

How Poison Came into the World (Choctaw). Other versions are found in *Native American Legends*, compiled and edited by George E. Lankford (Little Rock, Ark.: August House, 1987); and "Myths of the Louisiana Choctaw" by David I. Bushnell, *American Anthropologist*, No. 12, 1910).

The First Flute (Lakota). Versions in *American Indian Myths and Legends*, selected and edited by Richard Erdoes and Alfonso Ortiz (New York: Pantheon, 1984); and Eugene Buechel, *Lakota Tales and Texts* (Pine Ridge, S.D.: Red Cloud Indian School, 1978).

Munabozho and the Woodpecker (Anishinabe). Other versions are found in Alden O. Deming, *Manabozho* (F.W. David Co., 1938); and Henry R. Schoolcraft, *Algic Researches* (New York: 1839).

Why Coyote Has Yellow Eyes (Hopi). Other versions are found in Hamilton A. Tyler, *Pueblo Animals and Myths* (Norman: University of Oklahoma Press, 1975); Ekkehart Malotki, *Gullible Coyote* (Tucson: University of Arizona Press, 1985); and Mark Bahti, *Pueblo Stories and Storytellers* (Tucson: Treasure Chest Publications, 1988).

The Dogs Who Saved Their Master (Seneca). Versions of *Seneca Myths and Legends* by Arthur C. Parker, (Buffalo Historical Society, 1923); and *Seneca Fiction Legends and Myths* by J.N.B. Hewitt (Washington, D.C.: Bureau of American Enthology Bulletin 32, 1911).

Why Possum Has a Naked Tail (Cherokee). Other versions are found in Traveller Bird, *The Path to Snowbird Mountain* (New York: Straus and Giroux, 1972) and James Mooney, *Myths of the Cherokee* (Washington, D.C.: Bureau of American Ethnology Report 21, 1900).

How the Fawn Got Its Spots (Dakota). Other versions are found in *Legends of the Mighty Sioux* by South Dakota Writers' Project, 1941; and Eugene Buechel, *Lakota Tales and Texts* (Pine Ridge, S.D.: Red Cloud Indian School, 1978).

The Alligator and the Hunter (Choctaw). Other versions are found in *The Choctaw of Bayou Lacomb* by David I. Bushnell (Washington, D.C.: Bureau of American Ethnology 48, 1909); *Native American Legends* compiled and edited by George E. Lankford (Little Rock, Ark.: August House, 1987); and John R. Swanton, *Myths and Tales of the Southeastern Indians* (Washington, D.C.: Bureau of American Ethnology Report 88, 1929).

The Passing of the Buffalo (Kiowa). Other versions are found in Alice Marriott and Carol K. Rachlin, *American Indian Mythology* (New York: Mentor Books, 1968); and Alice Marriott, *Saynday's People* (Lincoln: University of Nebraska Press, 1963).

The Lake of the Wounded (Cherokee). Other versions are found in James Mooney, *Myths of the Cherokee* (Washington, D.C.: Bureau of American Ethnology Report 19, 1902); and Douglas A. Rossman, *Where Legends Live* (Cherokee, N.C.: Cherokee Publications, 1988).